NOVICE MAGEISTRA

EMPTY PROMISES

Heliotian Cycle : Book One

Lillian I. Wolfe

Published by Pynhavyn Press, Reno, Nevada

ISBN: 978-1-942622-37-6

The story, all names, characters, and incidents portrayed in this novel are fictitious. No identification with actual persons (living or deceased), places, buildings, and products is intended or should be inferred.

No generative AI was used to write this book.

This story was originally published on Vella as a serialized version. It has been edited with significant changes to the characters, world building and plot.

Dedication

This book first came to life a few decades ago and has undergone several changes and refinements over the years. It's the story that nagged until it found its proper place. I'd like to thank everyone over those years who read it, commented on it, and encouraged me to continue improving it. It is deeply appreciated.

-- Lily

Table of Contents

Chapter One 4
Chapter Two 15
Chapter Three: 25
Chapter Four 35
Chapter Five 48
Chapter Six 57
Chapter Seven 71
Chapter Eight 84
Chapter Nine 93
Chapter Ten 100
Chapter Eleven 111
Chapter Twelve 120
Chapter Thirteen 130
Chapter Fourteen 136
Chapter Fifteen 148
Chapter Sixteen 154
Chapter Seventeen 164
Chapter Eighteen 177
Chapter Nineteen 194
Chapter Twenty 203
Chapter Twenty-One 212
Chapter Twenty-Two 225
Chapter Twenty-Three 238
Chapter Twenty-Four 249
Chapter Twenty-Five 258
Chapter Twenty-Six 267
Glossary 280
RISING MAGEISTRA: RECALIBRATION 286
About the Author 297
Other Books by This Author 298

Arama

Arama is a world shaped by sunlight, fertile soil, and the steady rhythm of seasons that have sustained its people for generations. Its orchards, farmlands, and river valleys form the heart of a culture rooted in community and tradition, where life is measured in harvests and shared labor. Though peaceful in appearance, Arama holds a deeper significance in the Astara system—a place where destinies intersect and where the choices of a few may alter the future of many.

Corlan

Corlan, the moon-sized world that rises pale and constant in Arama's sky, carries the legacy of Arama's earliest inhabitants. When new settlers arrived, the first people crossed the void to Corlan, bringing their sciences, stories, and resilience with them. Smaller and harsher than the world they left behind, Corlan became a place of innovation and adaptation, its people shaped by memory and determination. Even now, Corlan's gaze toward Arama is one of connection, responsibility, and a history that binds the two worlds together.

ARAMA
BOWER
Nevis
LAKE Sila
Sila River
Ama City
AMA VALLEY
Elgin River
Dargon River
Tang
Wendford
Granner
KYR GLASS MTS
The Sisters
Mata
ARAMA

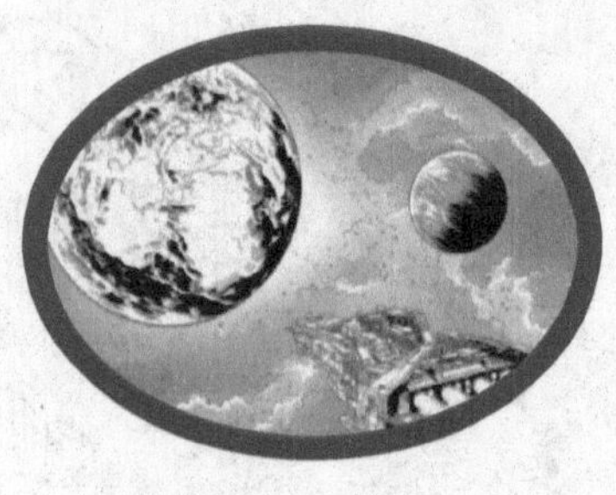

Chapter One

THE CHASE

THE SKIMMER SCREAMED ACROSS the moonlit fields, wind tearing at Cynara's hair. She leaned into the rush, crimson tunic billowing, silver strands whipping behind her like comet trails. The night was crisp, electric—too exhilarating for someone burdened with planetary duty.

She shouldn't enjoy this. Not with Arama in danger.

As Princess of Corlan, Cynara was sworn to protect the seven planets of the Astaran Consortium. Arama, the fertile heart of the system, fed them all. And something was poisoning it.

A flicker caught her eye—a glint of light near one of the dome-shaped farmhouses clustered to the east. She slowed her skimmer, a Royalist 100 coupe, and scanned the buildings. Moonlight had struck something metallic, but no farm equipment would be that reflective.

A frown creased her brow.

Then the air shifted.

A bulky skimmer burst from cover—a diplomatic cruiser, sleek and off-world in design. It surged toward her, engines whining.

Cynara didn't hesitate. She slammed the speed controls and veered toward Ama City. The cruiser wasn't local. Not Minoan. Not friendly. And on Arama, in the dead of night, that meant trouble.

She climbed to eight feet, banking left in a wide arc to shake pursuit. Her skimmer responded instantly, but the cruiser matched her move, closing the gap.

A strand of hair whipped into her eyes. She twisted to look back. The pursuer was less than twenty yards behind, its canopy down, its markings obscured. Whoever piloted it was good—too good.

She bit her lip and sealed her bubble canopy. Then she pushed the throttle to maximum and aimed straight for the city's outer wall.

They raced across the fields like twin wasps, engines screaming. Her skimmer began to lose ground, inch by inch. She coaxed it for more speed, but the engine refused.

"Sostana's curse on you," she muttered. "May your engine sputter."

Without breaking focus, she reached for the transmission unit. "This is Princess Cynara. I'm being pursued by an unidentified skimmer. I'll reach Ama City in two minutes. Activate dome shields on my signal."

The city wall loomed ahead—gleaming alloy, unforgiving. The cruiser still chased her, high-powered and relentless. Most diplomatic models couldn't match her ultra-speed coupe. This one could.

She considered turning to fight, but her offensive skills were untested. She couldn't risk it. Not yet.

A glance back showed the cruiser faltering. A plume of white smoke rose from its engine. It wasn't down, but it was slowing.

Good. That gave her a chance.

She approached the outer wall at full velocity. A second barrier stood just beyond it—two feet lower, barely a yard apart. Enough space for a skimmer. Barely.

Cynara angled in, cut speed to a quarter, then straightened her path. She elevated at the last moment, clearing the first wall by inches. Then she dropped between the barricades, skimming the narrow corridor at standard altitude.

She activated the shield signal.

A bluish-purple glow bathed the city's outer surface. The dome shimmered to life.

Cynara exhaled. The shield would stop her pursuer cold. By the time it disengaged, he'd have no idea where she'd gone.

She slowed, scanning for the entrance. Almost missed it. She swung hard, scraping the cushion guards against the left wall, narrowly avoiding a rear booster crash. Then she plunged into the tunnel's blackness.

The skimmer's lights flickered uselessly against the fog—thick, smudgy, unnatural. It wasn't just darkness. It was a kind of forgetting. The air grew colder, damp with the scent of moss and old stone. The walls pressed closer.

She slowed, relying on instinct. Even her instruments faltered here.

The passage twisted, then split. She veered left, then right, then left again. Had she passed this curve before? The skimmer's hum echoed strangely, as if the tunnel mocked her with her own sound.

Voices stirred in the silence. Not real ones—psychic echoes. Old minds, long gone, whispering through the stone.

She didn't let them in.

Another time, she'd listen. Tonight, she needed silence.

The tunnel narrowed, then widened. A gust of air brushed her cheek—cool, metallic, like breath from a buried machine. She pressed forward.

Finally, a dot of white light appeared ahead. Municipal corridors. Safety.

She passed through, beyond pursuit. No one could reach her apartments once the security field activated.

"Shield: three hours," she ordered.

The dome shimmered behind her, sealing the city.

She vanished into the fog, the voices in the tunnel stirring once more.

Not yet, she told them. Not tonight.

CYNARA PACED THE HARDWOOD floor of her reception chamber, boots clicking with each sharp turn. The fire crackled low in the hearth, its embers painting restless gold across the polished walls. Outside, the dome shield shimmered faintly, its bluish glow filtering through the high windows like moonlight caught in glass.

She had summoned Governor Rondu the moment she returned. Though he hadn't dared refuse her, she knew he'd arrive in a foul mood. She didn't care.

The poisoned river was worsening. Every day brought more damage to the Ama Valley. Seven days ago, the first signs appeared in Granner—a small village north of the Glass Mountains. The water turned a dull reddish hue. At first, no one noticed. Then the grasses wilted. The grain failed. Animals sickened and died.

Yesterday, a child died—wracked by cramps, drained by thirst, his small body finally surrendering.

Nineteen others showed symptoms. And the poison was moving, creeping downriver toward the sea.

She had stood on the banks three days ago, watching the red stain ripple through the reeds. The air had smelled wrong—metallic and sour, like rust and decay. Birds no longer sang there. Even the insects had fled. The silence was the worst part—as if the valley itself held its breath, waiting for the end.

If someone from the Astaran system—or worse, beyond it—had done this, what was the goal? What use was a dead world?

No answers. No logic. Just destruction.

Cynara felt sure the strange toxic potion flowing through their waterways came from beyond the Astaran Consortium, but so far, she had convinced no one else of her hypothesis. Governors, Clansmen, and the Kyerhala wanted verification.

At this point, all she could tell them was that the poison was unknown to any of their worlds. Even Corlan agreed, but it didn't discount the possibility that someone on Minos could have developed it. Since the Clan had never experienced aggression from another stellar system, they wouldn't consider the likelihood without proof.

Footsteps echoed in the corridor—heavy and measured. She dropped into the oversized chair near the fireplace, folding her legs and composing her expression. No weakness. Not in front of him.

The door slammed open.

"What is the meaning of this, Cynara?" Rondu barked, red-faced. His voice boomed with disdain. "Why summon me at such an indecent hour?"

Rondu was in his early nineties, his leathery skin etched with hundreds of wrinkles.

She regarded him calmly as she ran her hand over the padded arm of the chair. Trust Governor Rondu not to stand on ceremony.

"On my return from Sorcerer's Peak tonight, an off-world skimmer pursued me almost into the city."

"So? That is hardly cause to disturb my sleep." Rondu brushed his sleeve, symbolically dismissing her words.

She bit back her irritation, voice clipped. "Don't be a fool. You know off-world vehicles aren't normal on Arama. Why is one here, and where is it from? It didn't look like any design I've ever seen before, and I am familiar with all the Minoan models. Can you not see the implications?"

Scowling, Rondu searched for a chair, spotted a high-back in the corner, and pulled it over. Seating himself, he addressed her anew.

"Bata, you would know more about that than I. You, after all, are the royally educated sorceress—though I sometimes wonder if you paid any attention to the Clan trainers. Stati, young lady, your predecessor was much more hospitable. Prince Darius always had a warming drink waiting for an old man, and he would never summon me in the middle of the night. Then again, he often said nothing was so important that it could not wait for a decent hour."

"Yes, he would. But then, Prince Darius never had to cope with the threat of a worldwide disaster. Pity he died prematurely. I would rather he were here to handle this crisis—although I doubt he could have done much."

Rondu's face darkened with a scarlet flush.

Cynara knew Darius had been Rondu's good friend and protector. The man had often told her he had been but a youngster when the new sorcerer replaced old Prince Clementis, and they had become fast friends at once.

"Watch your tongue, young ruler. Prince Darius was a great sorcerer and a kind guardian. He was loved and admired. He set a fine example for others to—"

"He was a doddering old fool!" Cynara snapped, then caught herself. She was still young, barely sixteen years by Araman reckoning, and had little patience. "Governor Rondu, I realize that Prince Darius was an adequate guardian and that in your eyes I am not his equal. However, he is not here, and I am. I want the meager security guard we have on this palace increased. No unauthorized people are to be allowed entry. And block the city entrances of the ancient levels immediately."

"You mean the tunnels from the original walls? They're catacombs; no one could find his way through those—"

"I did, just a short while ago."

"Well, well, you must have some power after all," he sneered, as if her strength were nothing more than a parlor trick.

"And if I did," Cynara continued, refusing to be baited, "then someone with sophisticated instruments can as well. Close them!"

"If you were any kind of sorceress, you would erect a protective field around the city, and these precautions would not be necessary."

"Oh, Tiel, help me!" she groaned. "Everyone believes they know more about sorcery than those who practice it. I'm aware of what I can do. The only protective field able to surround us is a force shield. That requires a complete overhaul because my illustrious predecessor did not maintain it. I was fortunate it worked at all this evening."

She knew she'd stepped on Rondu's sensitive toes again—but she didn't care. Blame it on the old legends, making people believe Corlanish magic was so powerful it could do anything.

"Listen, child! I've had quite enough of this!" Rondu exploded, his face growing redder by the moment.

"I am not a child!" Cynara's fingers dug into the chair's arms, knuckles whitening as she forced herself to stay seated. Her wide, deep-blue eyes blazed. She was sixteen, but she had been trained for this. She would not let him rattle her.

"And I have had enough of you. Do you forget who you are addressing? You disregard the gravity of the situation. See to my orders at once. We don't have time to waste!"

To finalize the interview, she sprang to her feet and stalked from the chamber, leaving the governor staring open-mouthed after her.

If Rondu wouldn't act, she would—with or without him.

"Spoiled brat!" he muttered as she left, loud enough that she heard.

Cynara paused, fury burning in her chest. She despised the old man—but for now, she needed his cooperation.

Yet, a ball of flame coiled in her palm, its heat whispering temptation—just enough fire to remind him who she was.

Chapter Two

Seeking Answers

ANGER STILL COLORED CYNARA'S cheeks as she stalked into her private chambers, the door sliding shut behind her with a hiss. The firelight danced across the walls, casting long shadows that flickered like restless spirits. She barely noticed.

Being regarded as a child on this world was nothing new—but it still infuriated her. She'd never truly been one. Not on Corlan. Not in the eyes of the Clan. She'd been a small sorceress with adult responsibilities, trained to rule, shaped to serve. People like Rondu didn't understand that. They saw her age, not her burden.

She crossed to the window and stared into the night. Arama's sky shimmered with color—violet haze near the horizon, stars like scattered embers overhead. Corlan hung nearby, luminous and pale. It looked close enough to touch. Technically, it wasn't a moon but a sister planet, orbiting the red sun Astara alongside Arama. The true moon, smaller and silver-white, circled Arama and would soon eclipse Corlan in its race toward dawn.

She used to watch Arama from Corlan, wondering what life was like down there. She couldn't remember when the Clan teacher first told her she'd be responsible for it. It felt like she'd always known. What she hadn't known was how difficult, how exasperating, it would be.

A metallic clang snapped her attention back. Several objects floated midair—candlesticks, goblets, a scroll case—drifting in erratic patterns. A vase hovered near the far wall, trembling slightly.

She'd nearly hurled it.

Not the vase, she reminded herself. It was far too valuable, even if she despised it. Brash and grotesque, the ancient pottery radiated a sour energy. It always had. She exhaled slowly and willed it back to its pedestal, watching it settle with a faint hum.

Her telekinesis had flared again—uncontrolled, emotional. Rondu praised her predecessor's power, but Cynara knew the truth. She'd developed the ability young, and it had always been tied to her temper. Flying objects were her tell.

A soft growl pulled her gaze to the rug beside her bed.

Linhok stretched, snow-white fur rippling over powerful muscles. His green eyes gleamed with intelligence, the chiseled face half feline, half something more. A calculated crossbreed—frost leopard of Polara and Ergoan desert lion—he was graceful, lethal, and utterly loyal.

"Yes, Linhok," she murmured, smiling. "I lost control again. That horrid vase needs to go into storage."

Another growl, low and amused.

"I know. I'm not as patient as I should be. I hate this world. Especially that fool Rondu—though none of the governors are easy to work with. They don't see the danger."

Linhok rose and padded to her side, tail flicking. He reached her waist on all fours and could tear a man apart without hesitation. But with her, he was gentle. They'd been bonded since childhood—his telepathic voice one she'd never heard from another creature.

She scratched behind his ears, grounding herself in the familiar.

"What now?" she whispered, echoing his silent question. "I suppose I should contact Corlan. Maybe they can trace the skimmer."

Linhok growled softly.

"No, I'm not confident they'll identify it. I'm sure it came from beyond the Astaran system. But how it got here undetected…" She trailed off, rubbing his head. "I don't know."

What of your mission? Linhok's voice resonated in her mind.

She huffed a laugh. "I was so angry I didn't even tell Rondu. It went well enough, though. Lord Randoor promised help if things escalate.

His clan hasn't seen anything unusual in the Glass Mountains, but they'll keep watch."

The Kyreagle Clan. Native to Arama, older than the human tribes. Mostly birds, they bore a human-like face with a small beak and were quite intelligent. They'd once been fierce enemies. Wars, squabbles, uneasy truces. It had taken the Clan of Cantra to broker peace. Now, they were allies—barely. Cynara intended to keep it that way.

Good that they are alert, Linhok thought. She sensed his disappointment. He'd hoped for more.

She crossed to the wall panel and willed it open. The dark green board slid aside, revealing a blue plasma screen that shimmered to life. The sender-receiver unit was standard for Arama, but this one linked directly to Corlan. It could transmit voice, image, even constructed thought.

She didn't speak. She didn't need to.

Her memories transferred directly—the chase, the skimmer, the shield activation. Linhok watched the screen intently as she reconstructed the vehicle's design and requested identification.

After a long pause, a metallic voice responded: "No identification. Design not on record. Possible error in image transfer. Reconstruct again, please."

"Negative." Her voice was sharp. "No error occurred. Has anyone reported an unidentified space vehicle entering our solar system?"

"Negative."

"No reports of unusual activity?"

"Negative."

"Advise."

A new voice answered—calm, distant, familiar. A Clan watcher.

"Proceed with caution, Princess Cynara. Use your powers to look beyond yourself. We will continue to investigate. You must do likewise. May Tiel guide you."

"Tiel's grace," she answered with humility, and the panel slid closed.

Linhok growled, clearly unimpressed.

"No, it wasn't very informative," Cynara agreed. She walked to the window and sat on the sill, arms folded. Her gaze lifted to the sky.

Corlan glowed bluish purple, the moon a silver crescent preparing to eclipse it. Beyond them, stars glittered against the black—each a flame like Astara, each possibly surrounded by life-bearing worlds.

She remembered asking, as a child, if anyone lived out there. The Clan teacher had laughed. But there was a legend—settlers who came to Arama speaking a different tongue. That language had become the common speech here, distinct from Cantrese, the language of the Clan.

She'd learned both. Spoke both. But Araman still felt foreign.

A nudge at her arm. Linhok's growl.

"Look beyond yourself," the Clan watcher had said.

She rose and crossed the room to the curtained alcove. Linhok's eyes followed her, his mind-voice quiet but firm.

Must you?

Yes. I have no choice.

Guard my chamber well.

With a firm nudge against her hand, the sleek cat ambled to his station by the door and stretched out against it, his long body a silent barrier. Cynara forced herself to step forward. Her face showed no enthusiasm for the task—mouth a straight line, eyes fixed ahead. She parted the royal blue curtains just enough to slip through, then let them fall back into place behind her with a whisper of silk.

Inside the oval-shaped alcove, the air was thick—almost syrupy—with the pungent scent of almonwood. It clung to her throat, curled in her sinuses, and made her stomach churn. The incense was ancient, sacred, and overwhelming. It smelled of time itself—of dust and divinity, of rituals performed by generations long gone. It was the scent of Tiel, the all-powerful, the all-mighty.

She swallowed hard and stepped deeper into the gloom.

With deliberate motions, she raised her right hand, fingers trembling slightly as she stretched them outward. Power surged through her like a jolt of lightning—sharp, immediate, and alive. A blue-white flame burst from her middle fingertip, crackling softly in the still air.

Her hand moved in slow, practiced circles, tracing the ancient sigils of invocation. She touched the center candle of the seven-armed candelabra. The flame leapt from her finger to the wick, and the candle sparked to life with a glittering glow.

"The first is for Corlan," she intoned, her voice low and reverent, "the heart of the heavens, the world of the chosen."

She moved to the candle farthest left, then the one farthest right.

"Polara, the frozen world. Etoria, the burning land."

Another pause. Her hand hovered, then descended.

"Minos, the abode of science. Arama, the land of agriculture."

Finally, the last two.

"Ergos, the mineral world. Deca, the liquid world."

She lowered her hand, dropped her head, and sank to her knees on the woven mat. The flames flickered in unison, casting soft shadows across the alcove's curved walls.

Her eyes moved slowly across the space. The square altar stood before her, draped in a rich sky-blue cloth embroidered with silver thread. Behind it hung a tapestry—vivid and intricate—depicting the Astaran solar system in concentric rings of color and light. Each planet was stitched in its own hue, each orbit marked with symbols only the Clan could read.

To the side sat a small table bearing three ritual objects: a burnished golden bowl filled with fine brown powder, a silvery dish containing jagged purple crystals, and a linsar incense burner shaped like a coiled serpent.

The alcove held no carved statues, no towering icons. But it was sacred. Built into the royal apartments from the time of their construction, it had served as a temple to Tiel for every occupant since the first planetary guardian. It was quiet, intimate, and powerful.

Cynara had prayed here often. For guidance. For strength. For safety.

She did not like astral travel—this looking beyond oneself. But she had trained for it. She could do it with control. Most of the time.

It was exhilarating. It was terrifying. It was painful.

Her hand shook slightly as she reached for a pinch of the brown powder. She dropped it into the incense burner and touched the center candle's flame to it. The powder flared, releasing a fresh wave of almonwood smoke that curled upward in thick, oily tendrils.

Her nose wrinkled. She fought back a sneeze.

Next came the words—ritual phrases spoken in Cantrese, the sacred tongue of the Clan. She whispered them slowly, carefully, her voice barely audible over the crackle of flame. Some required intricate hand movements, and she performed them with precision, though she often wondered if they were more ceremony than necessity.

Then she reached for the purple crystals.

They were sharp to the touch, cool and humming faintly with stored energy. She placed two into the smoldering incense and sat back, hands resting lightly on her knees.

The crystals hissed as they met the heat. A violet fog began to rise—soft, shimmering, narcotic. It swirled around her, brushing her cheeks, seeping into her lungs. Her limbs grew heavy. Her breath slowed. Her mind began to drift.

She felt it first as a tickle—then a pull. The awareness of motion. Of rising.

Her astral-self twisted free, lifting upward through the fog toward the ceiling. She turned, instinctively, to look back.

Her physical body sat motionless on the mat. A slender, tanned young woman with silver hair and vacant eyes, bathed in purple mist.

She hated seeing herself this way. A shell. A husk. A vessel left behind.

But she had to look. She had to be sure the separation was clean.

Then she turned away and slipped through the ceiling like a wrath into the night.

The stars greeted her—cold, brilliant, endless. The dome shield shimmered below, a faint curve of light protecting the city. Beyond it, the poisoned river wound through the valley like a vein gone dark.

Somewhere out here, she needed to find answers.

Chapter Three

ENCOUNTERS TO THE EAST

"PRINCESS CYNARA MUST BE CAPTURED. As long as she is free, our plans can fail."

Governor Haburn swiveled his chair to face the alien woman seated across from him. His voice was firm, but his eyes betrayed unease.

"She has considerable powers," he continued, "as well as skill and cunning. But she is young. Unpredictable."

The Heliotian empress shifted in her seat, the movement subtle but telling. Her discomfort in the presence of Aramans was evident. Petite and raven-haired, she shimmered like a rainbow beetle—beautiful, but distinctly alien. Her orange-toned skin glowed faintly under the chamber's filtered light, and her dark eyes slanted upward above sharp cheekbones, unblinking and unreadable.

Her robe, woven in iridescent threads, overlapped a padded breastplate that gleamed with metallic accents. She was not here in peace.

"I agree with you, Haburn," she said, her accent thick, her words deliberate. "But it was your man who failed tonight. We merely provided the *ha-shar taraq*… the skimmer."

Haburn paled. He hadn't meant to offend. "Of course. I did not intend to suggest your people were at fault. I only meant to reiterate that we must take the sorceress if the planet is to come under our control."

The alien nodded, her expression unchanged.

"The organism will poison all life on this world in no more than four moon rotations," she said. "Helios does not wish to occupy a dead planet. Nor, I imagine, do you wish to govern a lifeless world."

Her voice was calm, clinical.

"If taking the girl hastens the defeat of the capital, then I favor such action. The sooner the city surrenders, the sooner we can destroy our toxic protozoa and allow the waters to resume their natural state."

Haburn steepled his fingers, trying to mask his nerves. "I would prefer to have Cynara in custody before we issue the ultimatum. She is the only one who can communicate directly with the Clan of Cantra."

"That is your responsibility, Haburn. The ultimatum must be issued within two sun cycles. Invent a reason to lure the princess into your trap. I leave that to you."

"Yes, Highness Y'riel. I will handle it."

He understood now—no additional help would come from the apricot-skinned Queen of Helios. Her tone made that clear.

He fidgeted under her gaze, tapping his fingertips together. Weak, her silence seemed to say. And Haburn felt the weight of her scorn.

"I fail to grasp your fear of this woman," she said at last, "or of the ones referred to as 'Clan of Cantra.'"

The door opened. Y'riel spared a glance for the man who entered.

Like her, his apricot-colored skin showed where his garments and helmet didn't cover. His dark eyes reflected no light. He snapped to a stiff pose just inside the door.

Haburn recognized him—Y'van, commander of the queen's occupation forces. Devoted. Dangerous.

"You speak as if these people possess mighty weapons," Y'riel continued. "Yet you say they do not. No guns. No cannon. Not even a sword. What is there to fear?"

Haburn wet his lips. He'd tried to explain this before.

"They have powers," he said. "Given by Tiel. They perform feats with their minds."

"Tiel?" Y'riel echoed. "Ah yes, your divine being. I do not understand that either. How can there be only one to worship? We honor many deities—most often revered ancestors."

She paused. "But no matter. Your people allege this princess possesses this gift of Tiel, yes?"

Haburn nodded.

"Then how did she escape your man by luck and quick thinking? Would she not have used her skills if she had any?"

She didn't wait for an answer.

"You may approach," she said to Y'van.

The soldier stepped forward, dropped to both knees, and extended his hands, palms up. Y'riel touched each with the pointed nail of her middle finger. On the second hand, she pressed harder, piercing the skin until a few drops of pale blood welled up. She dipped her head, then lifted the nail to her lips. A split tongue flicked out and licked it clean.

Haburn's stomach turned.

"*Visca na glic'ka*, Y'van," she murmured.

"Highness, the *ha-shar taraq* is returned. The oper'a'tive waits for interview. Is it your wish to be present?"

Her head shifted slightly. "It is not necessary. You will do what is required. Perhaps Governor Haburn would like to join you."

Haburn detected something unpleasant in her tone. He shuddered.

"As you wish, Highness."

He bowed stiffly and followed Y'van from the room.

DAMON MALTRON WAITED IN A square room with no windows, just a single door and a weak overhead light. Shadows pooled in the corners. Not exactly the reception chamber he was used to.

But then, he'd failed.

He sat up straighter as the lock clicked and the door opened. Y'van entered first, followed by Haburn. The alien warrior stood nearly a head shorter than Damon, but his presence was immense. Damon had seen him take down a much larger man with brutal efficiency. That was the moment Haburn had yielded.

"You mission fail," Y'van said, his Araman stilted and sharp. "Why?"

"The skimmer's engine stalled," Damon replied. "I almost caught her, but it sputtered out."

"Impossible." Y'van stomped the floor.

Damon didn't know if it was emphasis or threat. "It's what happened. I would've drawn even within thirty seconds if the power hadn't dropped."

Y'van's black eyes flared with a reddish glow. Damon held his gaze.

"The *ha-shar taraq* cannot 'drop power.' You pull back on it."

"I did not." Damon's voice remained calm. "I followed instructions. The unit sputtered."

"It cannot!"

"Something caused it to lose momentum. I didn't do anything."

Y'van's bone ridge flexed. His lips pulled back, revealing pointed teeth.

Haburn cleared his throat. "It might be the sorceress's work. She has the skill to cause such an incident."

Y'van turned on him. "Explain."

"She has magical power," Haburn said, flustered. "She can manipulate planetary forces."

Damon had no explanation. The indicators had read normal. The generator was active. But the engine had failed.

Y'van dismissed the theory. He stepped forward, pointing his bony middle finger at Damon's face.

Without warning, a stinger-like extension shot from his finger and pierced Damon's cheek.

Searing pain exploded through his face. He jerked back, legs pushing against the chair, but within seconds, his body went numb. Muscles refused to respond. He heard his own voice yelling, distorted and distant.

"You cause failure," Y'van said. "You work against Haburn?"

Damon tried to speak. “I… I work… for… him… not… scrap… job.”

Each word was agony. Sweat poured down his face.

He tried to focus on Y’van’s face, but everything blurred. Haburn’s voice echoed somewhere nearby, arguing, pleading. But the words didn’t stick.

Dizziness swept over him. The room tilted.

Then everything went black.

CYNARA’S ASTRAL-SELF SKIMMED OVER the land outside Ama City, retracing her dash to the walls. In this form, she saw the lingering energy trails from the two skimmers—hers a bright green streak, the other a curious shade of bluish-red. Not quite purple. Not a color signature used on Arama. Or any of the seven worlds.

She followed the trail as it retreated from the capital, noting how it backtracked, then veered east. She’d encountered it three hours after leaving the western mountains, just past the Dangon River. But she hadn’t seen where it came from.

The residue thinned as she tracked it. Odd. It should’ve been stronger—more recent. She dashed ahead, following the fading trail as it curved toward Tark Lonan, the largest city in the South Division.

She willed herself there.

In seconds, she hovered above the city's skyline, the buildings glowing faintly under the dome shield. If only physical travel worked as efficiently as astral projection, she could be anywhere, anytime. But as a spirit, she could only observe.

She swept through downtown, scanning for the skimmer. Her senses were hyper-attuned—every light, every motion registered. The government building stood tall, its windows lit even at this hour. Strange. She'd met Governor Haburn before. Adequate, if uninspired. Not the type to work late.

She considered slipping inside—no one could see her in this form—but her focus remained on the unknown vehicle.

A quick loop around the government grounds revealed no sign of it. The city's fleet was parked behind the structure, orderly and unremarkable.

She widened her search, following traffic lines outward. Most vehicles left faint trails, but none matched the bluish-red signature. Then she spotted the spaceport to the north—a sprawling complex shaped like a twelve-pronged molecule, with a central dome and radiating arms.

She blinked there instantly.

Three space shuttles sat on the west side, workers bustling around them. Cargo loaders hummed. Lights flickered. Routine.

But on the east side, one building stood out—an oblong warehouse, unlike the others. Its shape broke the symmetry of the port.

She zipped closer, slipping through the wall like mist.

Inside, a single fixture cast dim light over a dark blue space shuttle. Sleek. Interplanetary. But not Araman. Not Consortium-made. Not anything she'd seen before.

She drifted down, circling the vessel. Its hull shimmered with unfamiliar alloys. The design was angular, predatory. The markings—if they were markings—glowed faintly in a script she didn't recognize.

None of it came from the seven worlds of Astara.

She rounded the front—and froze.

An orange-skinned figure stood beside the shuttle. Tall, armored, alien. Something resembling a laser rifle rested across its arms. Its helmet bore a pointed crest, sharp and insectile, like a bee's stinger.

It turned.

Black eyes above sharp cheekbones, unblinking, and unreadable locked onto her.

She panicked. It shouldn't be able to see me!

She darted upward, toward the roof.

The alien raised its weapon.

A streak of energy shot through the air—crackling, violet, fast.

It passed through her—but not harmlessly. Her essence rippled, her vision blurred. Pain flared—not physical, but psychic. A jolt of disruption.

She burst through the ceiling, rising into the night sky, heart pounding in her chest though her body lay far away.

It saw me.

It fired.

It knew.

Chapter Four

PLANS REACHING FOR FRUITION

THE SAW-BACK SHUTTLE angled upward through the atmosphere toward an unseen destination in deep space. On the transceiver, an insistent bleep guided it to a rendezvous point with the Heliotian support ship, waiting beyond the reach of any scanners in the solar system. Cloaking kept the vessel invisible, the steady signal its only tether to the star cruiser.

At one of the two unshielded portholes, Empress Y'riel sig Die'hla, exalted High Queen of the Heliotian Empire, stared unwaveringly at the blue-green ball shrinking behind them.

Soon, it would be hers—the first of this star cluster's worlds to fall under her rule. Colonies would spread across the Astaran system, with at least three planets habitable without domes. Four others already sustained life under giant bubbles, a technology that still amazed her. Compared to the overcrowded Helios system, where her people fought for every inch of space and morsel of food, Arama seemed a paradise.

"How did this backward race ever venture into space, let alone build those life domes on hostile planets?" she mused aloud.

Y'van, piloting, answered in their harsh tongue. "Perhaps they had help."

"Help? From where? No other life-supporting stars are closer than Helios. Apart from this system, we have detected no others."

Y'riel turned her gaze toward Corlan, the heart-world of the Astaran group, home of the so-called Clan of Cantra. Haburn feared their mental abilities; if his concerns proved valid, they would have to be eliminated.

She settled back against the cushions, prepared for the long journey to the support ship. Ten or twelve cycles would see the culmination of her plan. She had approached Haburn nearly eight Araman divisions ago, after two periods of careful study. Once she determined Arama would be the first target, infiltrators evaluated the situation. An emissary found Haburn ambitious, easily swayed by promises of power.

Several meetings followed, including a trip to Hatara, one of the Heliotian Empire's two worlds. There, Haburn saw their technological might firsthand. Convinced of their superiority, he yielded, his price only the Governorship of Arama.

With his help, they established a laboratory at the base of the Glass Mountains, where the

Dangon River broadened into the Ama Valley. The agricultural region surrounding Ama City was key. Into its waters they released microscopic organisms—harmless themselves, but their waste combined with water to form a potent poison.

"How long to docking?" she asked.

"Navigation estimates five *m'arsk*s, mar *Hel'talek*." Y'van studied the readout. "The support ship is still screened."

"Good. Instruct them to remain so until we are a few su'biz from docking. I don't wish to risk anyone seeing our ship."

Y'van laughed drily, black eyes sparkling. "What could they do? These planets have no defenses—unless you believe Haburn's tale of sorcerers protecting the system."

"Of course not." A smile touched her lips. "But it disturbs me they show no resistance. How is there such poor control in a system with five inhabited worlds? Imagine if Hatara had no defenses."

"We would have been annihilated centuries ago."

"Exactly. We are constantly warring. Yet if reports are true, there hasn't been a war here in over eight hundred h'yni. They maintain a small population without controls. Studying this society will be… very interesting—especially the Clan of Cantra."

She leaned back, aiming to sleep before docking. Her thoughts turned again to the plan: first, water poisoning by the controlled organism timed to die in thirty days. The people would panic, unaware of its short lifespan, and beg their leaders for protection.

Next, Haburn would hand Tark Lonan over in a public ceremony, no fight required. Then Ama City would fall—small ships and laser cannons if necessary—to demonstrate military power. With those three moves, she felt confident the planet would surrender. Once Arama fell, the others would follow.

If the Clan or the sorceress had any means to resist, they would deal with it. So far, no evidence of power, no defenses beyond crude shields. Tark Lonan's force field could be punctured with a disrupter, allowing warriors to demolish its source.

Confident, Y'riel tipped her seat back. The three steps of domination had worked on two other worlds her father had taken. They would yield victory here.

Before she drifted off, she mumbled, "If their only defense is a half-trained sorceress and crude shields, then they are already defeated. Empires never fall to such weakness—only to arrogance. But arrogance, of course, is something we have mastered."

A SMALL FIRE BURNED in the hearth, sending elongated shadows climbing the curved walls. With ill-concealed impatience, Travis waited as his mother served hot osang and berry cakes to everyone seated in a semi-circle before the fire. Travis shifted his weight again, and his mother's smoke-gray eyes shot a warning glance his way. He stared down uneasily at the floor, wishing the celebration was over, and he was on his way.

Lifting his cup of osang toward the fire, his father requested Tiel's blessings for his house and those in it. Travis reflected it was the same blessing he'd heard every night of his life, not even one word of variation. While he might miss this ritual, he welcomed the change. The small gathering included his family and a few close friends from the area who'd come together to wish him a safe journey to Weilock Center.

Cautiously, he sipped at the steaming drink, still trying to accustom his tongue to the full strength of the sunberry wine. Until his eighteenth birthday, he'd always drunk watered-down osang, just as his younger brother Brandon still did. He hadn't decided if he liked it full strength.

Across from him, his grandfather watched in amusement, almost as if he could read Travis's mind. Brandon stared greedily at the slice of cake on his brother's plate, then finally asked, "Are you going to eat your cake, Travis?"

"No, you can have it." Travis glanced toward his younger brother, a smaller version of himself and their mother. Brandon would be thirteen soon, and he was already better with a horse than Travis was. In all likelihood, he would turn out to be a better farmer since the kid enjoyed the lifestyle.

Travis sensed his father's eyes on him as Garrett DeLonge studied his boys, no doubt seeing two strong young men with sun-streaked brown hair and tanned faces and arms from working in the sun all day. He wore an expression of puzzlement, as if he didn't recognize his older son. Uncomfortable under the scrutiny, Travis shifted his position and looked away.

"A salute," Garrett said, "to my brilliant son, who earned a university education despite his old man. The brains must come from his mother's side of the family, don't you think, Granddad?"

The old man nodded in agreement, poured himself another glass of osang, and proceeded to get happily inebriated on the potent wine.

With a shy grin of thanks, Travis glanced across the room at a somewhat tall, sturdily built young girl who sat silently watching him, a mixture of emotions evident on her face. He'd known Dawnha all his life, had grown up with her tagging along everywhere he went. She'd been his partner at the numerous dances at Wendford, the small town serving this community of farms. As much as he would miss her company, he knew she would miss him even more. But the time for a break had come. He snapped out of his thoughts as he realized someone had asked him a question.

Siri Fratain beamed down at him and asked him what he planned to study at the "fancy university."

"Engineering and design," Travis replied. "I tested well in those areas, and I sent a few designs I'd created with the test."

"Engineering," Fratain scoffed. "What'ta ya goin' to do with engineering on a farm? All ya need to know is how to fix the 'bots or the tractors, and ya already know that."

"Yes, sir," Travis agreed affably. "But maybe, when I'm done learning, I might be able to improve the designs of some agricultural machinery or build a self-repairing 'bot."

"Yeah, now you do that, lad, and this university might be beneficial after all." Chuckling, Fratain refilled his glass and moved along to speak with Travis's father. He overheard him say something about the new grain from the Minoan Agricultural Department.

Most farmers didn't think much of a university education, Travis reflected, but then he didn't intend to stay a farmer. He might design better 'bots, but most of his thoughts leaned toward developing faster, more fuel-efficient shuttles and continuing his education on Minos.

He hesitated, then added quietly, "This morning I saw something in the sky—silver, streaking east. Not Minoan. I know their designs, and this one was different. Sleeker, almost like a squid with a fin running its length."

His father's brow furrowed. "Probably a shuttle," he said, though his voice carried unease. "Strange things pass overhead sometimes. Best not dwell on them."

Dawnha's eyes flicked toward him, her expression tightening. "Always looking to the skies, Travis," she said softly, almost to herself. "No wonder you're leaving us behind."

Her words carried more weight than she might have intended, but Travis caught the sting. He opened his mouth to reply, then closed it again, unsettled. The image of the silver ship lingered, now tangled with the ache of parting.

Again, his gaze returned to Dawnha, who stared down at the nearly full glass of osang she held in her hand. Her long brown hair was braided and wrapped in a swirl at the back of her neck. Travis thought about how smooth and silky it was when it hung free, so his hands could sift through it. The hairs on his neck tickled, and he turned to find his mother's eyes on him. When she'd caught his attention, she shifted her eyes to Dawnha and arched an eyebrow. Understanding, Travis nodded his agreement, set his own glass down, and went to talk to her.

Dawnha looked up to him, her eyes a dark, watery blue as she appeared to be near tears. He offered his hand. "Let's go for a walk."

They slipped out of the room, unnoticed except by Alia, his mother, who offered a sympathetic smile when he glanced back at her.

"Why do you need to go?" Dawnha asked after they had walked a fair distance from the dwelling and were practically in the almon tree grove. "Don't you have all you need here?"

Travis wrapped his arm over her shoulders, pulling her close to him. The fresh almon soap scented her hair, the light fragrance stimulating his senses. He stopped and turned her to face him. "No, Dawnha. I know this is hard for you, but I don't have everything I need here. I have ideas, and my plans can only be realized if I go to the university. My life doesn't really begin until I can make those ideas reality."

"But what about me, Travis? Don't I mean anything to you?"

He saw the plea in her eyes, the tremble of her lips, and recognized the need for him to say he wanted to stay with her.

"Of course, you mean a great deal to me. You've been my closest friend from the time we could barely walk. You'll always be special, and I'll send you messages. But I have to go, Dawnha. I don't know when, or even if, I'll be back here." He found this farewell more difficult than he considered it would be.

"Shall I wait for you, then?"

"No!" He said it too quickly, too sharply. "I mean, don't count on me coming back to you. Look for your own happiness, my friend. You'll make a wonderful partner for a farmer around here. You know Josah keeps eyeing you."

"I see," she answered, looking away from him. "You've always worshipped those damn stars, dreamed of them—and now, you're leaving me to go to them. How can I fight such a rival?" She turned her face to him, the tightness of her features telling him she was fighting back the tears. "Well, I wish you good luck, Travis DeLonghe."

As he reached to pull her close in a hug, she stepped away, shook her head. "And I don't want Josah for a mate!" She darted back toward the house in a hasty run. Travis started to go after her, ran a few steps, and stopped. It was best to let her go. She would handle the breakup in her own way. He knew no easy path to tell the girl who loved him he didn't feel the same, but he wished he could have said it better.

Gazing up at the few wisps of clouds above him, he remembered the strange silver streak he'd seen at dawn. The image unsettled him, but he pushed it aside, focusing instead on his dream: one day his own shuttle, a fast-moving bird of metal, would streak across a solar system at double their speed. Perhaps farther, to search for other worlds. That was his dream, to reach beyond these seven little planets to find more.

Even though it was late when he finally returned to the house, several lights still burned. After a moment, he pushed the door open. His mother waited for him by the fire.

"Sit down, Travis," Alia said softly, yet her authority would accept no argument. He nodded once, then sat. She studied her son's face, reached across, and touched his cheek with the back of her hand, as she had done ever since he was a small child. "I'll get you a cup of osang."

He shook his head. "No, thanks, Mom. I've had enough tonight to last me for a while."

"Hot tea, then? You're chilled."

"Okay," he agreed quietly, knowing she'd go through every available hot drink until he accepted one. He wished she would just go to bed and let him do the same. With a long trip ahead of him, he intended to get an early start. He'd decided to see some sights on the way, so he was taking the wagonner instead of a skyhopper from Bay Cross.

His mother held out a cup, which he accepted and sipped. He silently admitted the tea tasted good and offered some comfort.

Alia waited a few moments, then asked, "Your talk with Dawnha didn't go well, did it?"

He shook his head.

"She doesn't want to wait for you to finish school?"

"I didn't ask her." At her sharp look, he added, "It wouldn't be fair to her. I don't love her—at least, not the way she wants—and I don't plan to partner with her. Besides, I could be gone a long time."

"I suspected as much. You aim to continue with your learning, then? Go to another world?"

He could never bluff when it came to dealing with his mother. "It's what I want. If I'm good enough, I'll have the opportunity." He hadn't told his parents the Weilock Center University was only a training stop, and Minos's Engineering College had already accepted him.

Alia rose, touched his cheek gently. "We'll miss you, Travis, but you must do what is in your heart."

In a rare display of affection, Travis kissed his mother's cheek before bidding her good night. It would be the last time for a while. Saddened by the thought, he headed for the bedroom he shared with Brandon. His younger brother couldn't wait to have the room for himself.

Chapter Five

AN EXPLOSIVE SITUATION

BOLTING FROM HER CHAMBERS, Cynara ran down the hallway to her suite's entrance. Linhok, his claws scraping against the tile, skittered around the corner on her heels. Beyond the door, her chamber's guard crouched on alert with his weapon drawn.

"What was that explosion?" she yelled as she approached.

The cat sniffed the air, his head turning to find the scent.

Alder lifted his communicator. "Waiting for word, your Highness. It sounded like it came from the north."

Eastern wall. Linhok responded. *I smell limestone and ferigout.*

"East." Cynara's voice was clipped, certain. "The old wall's weaker. Someone's trying to break through. Call the watch on the eastern wall.

Alder responded immediately.

She trusted Linhok's nose over Alder's guess. Only the eastern defense contained ferigout in its composition. The reddish iron ore had been a gift from the northerners when the initial construction commenced two centuries ago.

The communicator crackled. Alder listened, then nodded. "Just five meters short of the Iron Gate. Minimal damage although it beached the first layer."

"I'm on my way." Cynara tapped Linhok's shoulder, and they loped toward the city transport vehicles.

Cynara halted the city skimmer a few yards from the small crowd of guards and curious onlookers at the wall. Broken stone littered the ground, dust still hanging in the air. Linhok's growl cleared a path faster than the soldiers could. The locals retreated at the sight of the frost leopard. The crowd buzzed with excitement and her presence. Not fear. Cynara frowned. Were they reassured by the military presence or blind to the danger?

She didn't share their confidence, although she believed no one would hang around after setting it off. She strode forward as Captain Ershell came forward to address her.

"Your Highness." He saluted her. "The blast ruptured the exterior wall with a two-meter opening."

Stepping around the debris, Cynara moved closer, eyes narrowing at the jagged opening. Large enough for a person to slip through. A dozen footprints marked the dust-covered ground. Any could be from the perpetrator. If someone had entered the wall, he could be making his way toward the armory in the north or to the power generators at the gate. *Linhok?*

The cat crouched, and leaped through the gap, his pads thudding into the space between the walls. The thumps on the ground faded as he raced to the north.

Cynara turned to Ershell. "Has anyone checked for the intruder inside the walls? Are your troops alert to the possibility someone has broken into the city?"

Like the passageway she'd used to slip into the city earlier, all fortifications had dual barriers. While the front entry was a maze, the north and east walls encompassed only one set.

"My troops are investigating." He pointed to the footprints. "But townsfolk arrived first, rummaging through the damage. No one saw anyone."

With a sharp nod, Cynara stepped to the opening, reaching out with her senses. She closed her eyes and extended her hand over the area. Movement, voices, but none from within. Opening her eyes, she snapped her fingers, conjuring a globe of light that floated into the gap. She climbed the unstable blocks, stepped into the dark well between the walls, and peered down, eyes seeking footprints or any other evidence someone had entered. Apart from the leopard's paw prints, she didn't see anything. Linhok covered the armory, so she turned toward the gate and the power plant, her light floating a meter in front of her.

A pair of soldiers followed her, their boots scraping on the stone. *Good to know I have protection.* Aloud, she said, "Stay close. I'm not sensing danger yet, but there could be some. Is anyone going to the north?"

"Yes, Highness," a woman's voice answered.

Relief lightened her spirit. Linhok had backup. His thoughts brushed hers. *All is clear thus far. Halfway to the armory.*

Be cautious.

Always.

A wicked smile curved her lips. Linhok searched in hunting mode, using every sense he had to detect anything awry. So should she. She inhaled deeply, wrinkling her nose at the stench of vermin, undaunted by the sealed passages.

About twenty feet farther, she picked up an unfamiliar odor. Halting, she directed her light toward the inside wall and her eyes darted along with it, looking for the source. The glow barely illuminated the dark-colored package taped to the interior surface. She pointed it out to the woman behind her. "Looks like an explosive. Can you identify it?"

The soldier stepped in front of her, pulled out a vision enhancer, and peered through it. "Yes, a Minoan blast cap, Highness."

"Can you defuse it?"

She shook her head. "It's a remote construction blaster. Blocking the signal would be difficult before it explodes. I see a motion detector, so if you even get too close, it will trigger the device."

Cynara caught her breath in a shallow gasp. "Go back now. It's a trap." *Get out of your side, Linhok.*

Cynara spun around and raced for the opening. The perpetrator had covered their tracks well and set explosives inside the passages. She figured it wasn't to break through into the city, but an attempt to kill her or whoever came to investigate.

She urged her two guards ahead of her, pausing to cast a force shield behind them, blocking the tunnel. She'd scarcely activated it when the blast roared through the passage, shaking the ground like a violent earthquake.

She and the two soldiers with her went tumbling, arms and legs twisting. Cynara's body thudded into something as her head smacked against it. Her vision cleared and she gazed back toward the explosion. The shield had stopped any flying debris and the deadly force from reaching them.

My lady! Are you injured?

Linhok's urgent voice cut through Cynara's dazed mind. Pain shot through her back and hip when she tried to move, and she realized the blast had thrown her into the wall. *Here, Linhok. Banged up. How are you?*

"Your Highness?" the woman soldier called out. "Are you hurt?"

"I don't think so. Give me a minute. What about you?"

"We're battered, but alive," a man's voice answered, grunting through the pain.

"Take your time. Your names?"

"Sgt. Greza," the woman replied. "And my partner is Marksman Kalmet."

"I'm glad you survived." Cynara forced herself up to sit against the wall, breathing through the aches.

Linhok's voice came through again. *Safe. One soldier is badly injured. They could not run as swiftly.*

Are you out?

I am. Others are seeing to the injured man. Shall I come to you?"

Kalmet stumbled to her and offered his hand. "Do you need help, Highness?"

She accepted and allowed him to pull her up. She wobbled a little, trying to get her feet under her. Minor pain, nothing to indicate a severe injury, she concluded. Stepping to the point, she and her escort limped toward the opening again, where Captain Ershell hurried to meet them.

"Thank the stars, you're alive." Relieved, he stepped to Cynara's side, offering his arm for support. "Your leopard came out moments before the explosions."

Ignoring his assistance, she plodded ahead, anxious to exit. "I heard one of your people was injured. How bad?"

"A broken arm, cuts, and a possible concussion. He was a minute behind the cat. Are you injured? I'll call a medic."

"I am fine, Captain. See to your people." Her headache and the soreness diminished once she started moving. She'd take a healing draught when she returned to her chambers.

Then Linhok telepathed a new warning. *Rondu is here.*

Of course, he was. Anything that might draw a crowd brought out the governor. He was probably berating her already. She clambered through the opening and blinked against the morning sun.

"And here she is now," Rondu proclaimed loudly. "Have you secured the perpetrators, your Highness?"

He pivoted toward her, displaying a sharp-as-blade smile. She itched to knock the leer off his face but contained her annoyance. "Whoever it was is long gone; however, they left behind a nasty pair of surprises." Linhok padded to her side, a low growl rumbling. She placed a calming hand on his shoulder. "We were lucky to spot the blast caps before they triggered."

Rondu arched an eyebrow. "Fortunate, indeed. Do you suppose it was one of your 'aliens'?"

"At this point, I draw no conclusions. The devices appeared to be Minoan construction. I expect a full investigation." She turned to Ershell. "See that it's done, Captain."

"Of course, your Highness." He stepped away to see to her orders .

"If you have nothing else, Governor, I wish to return to my chambers." She stepped past him, Linhok at her left side, when Rondu spoke again.

"Remember, the council meeting begins at ten hours this morning. Shall we expect you?"

She shot a glare at him. "I will be there." Straightening her shoulders, she plunged past, the regal pair cutting a path through the onlookers.

She needed to notify Corlan of everything she'd learned, report this latest incident, then try to get a quick nap in before the meeting. If she could postpone the council, she would, but she must attend. The matters being addressed were too important.

The timing troubled her—last night's pursuit, this morning's blast. Was it a breach attempt, or bait meant to draw her into danger? She doubted an alien planted the device, but allies on Arama seemed certain.

Do you suspect Rondu? Linhok asked.

Possibly, but what would his motive be? To eliminate me? He dislikes me but killing me would leave this world in jeopardy. Corlan doesn't have a replacement ready. Rondu might be a greedy, despicable man, but would he sell out the planet to an alien race? I don't think so, but someone else might do it.

As she strode away from the wall, Linhok pacing at her side, Cynara's thoughts congealed. The explosion had been no random act; it was a calculated strike, meant to test her authority and the city's defenses. She lifted her chin, forcing her stride into regal steadiness despite the ache in her back. If they think I will be frightened into silence, they are mistaken.

The council would hear her voice today, and Corlan would have her report. Whoever aided the aliens—whether Rondu, Haburn, or another hidden hand—she would uncover them. And when she did, the conspirators would learn that the sorceress they dismissed as weak was far from defenseless.

Chapter Six

FIFTEEN POLITICIANS AND A PRINCESS

"WE MUST BUILD UP OUR DEFENSES."

Though softly spoken, the words rolled through the domed chamber, built so even a whisper carried. The fifteen governors, or their representatives, huddled together, conspiratorial in tone. The man who'd spoken was Trasarth, a middle-aged tradesman from Sant Olga on the northeast coast. He adjusted his stance and threw his thin shoulders back to bolster his position.

Arms folded over her chest, Cynara stood at the back of the chamber, leaning against the wall and listening, unnoticed. The debate had dragged on for nearly an hour.

Shortly after she'd assumed her position on Arama, she'd found this little spot in the chamber where she could watch and hear unobserved. The shadow of one of the domed support beams concealed her presence. She often learned more by eavesdropping than the councilmen would ever admit face-to-face. She'd listened to most of Trasarth's dissertation, an attempt to motivate the others to act.

Governor Rondu sprang to the floor. “Defenses against what? Poison in the water? You’re beginning to sound like the Clan sorceress—seeing threats that don’t exist. The only thing threatening us is an unknown toxin in our river water. There could be dozens of reasons, and researchers on Minos are studying samples that will, in due time, tell us what it is and how to clear it up.” Rondu shrugged dismissively. “In the meantime, the Clan of Cantra provides any other protection we might need.”

“Rondu is right,” another councilman, the representative from Weilock Center, interjected. “We are probably worrying needlessly—”

“Needlessly, gentlemen?” Trasarth interrupted. “You say we worry needlessly, yet the lands that feed half our system are dying. How long until Minos discovers the reason? A few days? A few weeks? How long will our lands last? And what about the explosions at the northeast wall this morning?”

Holding fast to his belief, Rondu waved a dismissive hand. “The explosions are unrelated. As to the other, the Clan of Cantra will—”

“The Clan of Cantra will save you,” Cynara cut in, striding toward the council. “Just like all the legends, they will descend from their temple and sweep away any danger. Good day, gentlemen."

Rondu's eyebrows bristled, and he prepared himself for battle. "Ah, here is the young guardian of our planet now. We're pleased you could join us. This meeting was your idea, was it not? Are you, in your quaint fashion, attempting to tell us the Clan will not help us?"

"Most assuredly not, Governor. I am merely suggesting you not depend solely on them. They will do everything within their powers to aid this world—as will I—but our unique capabilities may not reach the source of this problem. You would do well to heed Trasarth's advice." With a sweeping motion, she shifted her long gown to one side and seated herself across from Rondu.

"That's preposterous!" Rondu sputtered. "Trasarth is advising we build up defenses. What defenses would you recommend? There is no threat, nothing to defend against. We have food stores and ample water to support the entire population of Arama for a full division. What more is there to do?"

"One division—twenty-eight days—is hardly long at all." Cynara tilted her head back and stared up at the curved roof. When she spoke again, her voice was very soft and filled with undeniable sadness. "And what about the animals and the fish? They will be dead before the end of the first division—precious lives we might still save. New crops can be started with seeds, but it will take many divisions. Even more to get the few representatives of each specimen in suspension on Minos to breed and give birth to new animals and fish. Then it takes more time to grow the herds large enough again to provide food. And there's the matter of a child already dead from the poison—and who knows how many more before we find the antidote?"

For several long minutes, silence hung in the room while each of the men absorbed the full impression generated by the quiet voice of the sorceress. Was it prophecy or merely the musings of a young girl? Uneasily, one councilman cleared his throat. "It seems to me it would be foolish not to breed these animals on planets other than Minos for contingency. Why hasn't the Clan provided for that?"

Bringing her eyes to rest on the man, a bald, squint-eyed farmer from Tark Noter on the eastern plateau, Cynara blinked, and her voice took on a deep, business-like tone. "Have you seen the other planets in our solar system, Councilman Harga? The animals we raise here could not survive on those worlds. Perhaps one or two species could adapt, but not the majority. All our worlds are far too different. Where our people have adjusted, the animals failed to adapt, although it has been tried. A few unique animals resulted—like the freparda and the zelebras. But none of those are food species. Like the people living on those worlds, the animals need a controlled environment. Finally, the domed cities are simply not large enough for livestock. While a few species live on Ergos, most simply will not adapt.

"No, I'm afraid the only creatures living on the other planets are the ones native to them. However, to answer your question, Governor Rondu, we must be prepared to defend ourselves against the individuals who are responsible for the poison. It didn't just happen. Rest assured, whoever is behind it will show themselves before this world is dead. That is a certainty."

"Have you returned to your 'alien theory,' Princess?" Rondu asked, his tone sour enough to drip, with a sneer.

"I never left it." She wanted to add she'd seen proof, but not yet. She wouldn't reveal it until she had more information.

"You truly believe life from beyond our system would invade? It is the most ridiculous thing you've said so far. All you need to do is look at our other planets to realize how slim the chances of intelligent life developing outside our system are. Can you imagine a Cetus—or any so-called intelligent marine life of Deca—attacking another planet?" He laughed, and several of the councilmen joined in.

"How about a dragora?" a voice piped up, and another wave of laughter swept the room at the thought of one of the pig-sized, horned lizards of Minos trying to take over anything.

"And no one would dare attack against the Clan of Cantra if they had any knowledge of this world," Haburn continued, mocking her. "Why, no one would even dare to challenge you, and your powers are but a fragment of a true lord. If you are afraid, perhaps you should request assistance."

An ominous silence hung in the room while Cynara's face flushed in anger. She struggled to control her temper. Abruptly, a pitcher shuddered and skittered down the table, weaving side to side.

Oh, hellfire, Cynara thought, dismayed she couldn't control her telekinesis when she was angry. She fought to regain control as it teetered at the edge, nearly emptying its contents into Rondu's lap before she mastered herself. She turned her fury inward, ashamed she'd let emotion slip its leash. The pitcher ceased to move, and no other objects took flight.

Trasarth, along with the others, had watched this knee-jerk reaction with a mixture of amusement and awe. Nonetheless, Rondu outright questioned the competency of the guardian of Arama. Although he might do so privately, bringing it up in the council chamber was highly improper. Cynara caught the look of dismay on Trasarth's face and knew the minor bit of telekinesis had likely cost her some goodwill among a few representatives.

"I believe you spoke unwisely, Governor Rondu," Trasarth said. "Princess Cynara is more knowledgeable in these matters, and I, for one, would like to hear her ideas. You owe her—and this council—that courtesy, regardless of your feelings."

"It's all right, Councilman," she said with composure, putting the unfortunate incident behind her. "I am aware of Governor Rondu's feelings in this matter, and perhaps what I suggest is difficult for a mind..." She paused, searching for the right words. "...too set in its own way to accept. My thinking does not parallel Prince Darius's, with whom Governor Rondu worked so closely. As far as my theory goes, it is little more than speculation unless you count the extra senses I sometimes get. What I believe, gentlemen, is an alien force is behind our poison problem. One reason is because we cannot identify the toxin. Minoan biologists are working on it but frankly admit they have observed nothing else like it, although they believe it to be organic. Last night I sensed an intelligence equal—or greater—than ours. I don't feel we can discount the possibility because we've never encountered it before."

Cynara waited, her bright eyes gliding from one face to another, appraising their reactions. What she saw in the silent expressions was little more than she'd expected. Like Rondu, they found the suggestion of other life in the universe unthinkable. Still, they paid her the courtesy of not laughing outright at her. They would do it later when they met for dinner and exchanged viewpoints. She sensed the struggle when Trasarth tried to give respect to her suggestion. If the situation weren't potentially dangerous, the whole thing would be amusing.

"It is difficult to accept the idea," Trasarth finally said, dragging the words out as if he hoped they would transfer themselves into the proper response. He refused to meet her eyes; instead, he engaged the ones of the councilman from Weilock Center.

With a short laugh, Cynara saved him further embarrassment. "Indeed, it is difficult to accept, and I can understand that. We did not teach the people of our solar system to look beyond our own star for life. Our scientists never developed interstellar spacecraft, nor did we attempt to seek life beyond Astara. Still, I believe it is there, and it is about to find us. So, even if you don't believe my theories, what harm is there in being prepared for the worst? All the major cities possess defensive shields even though most are like Ama City's—needing repair. At least, we can make those functioning again. By the way, did you ever wonder why we have the shields?"

"But the Clan will prevent an invasion—if one were to happen," a short round man named Loring objected. The alternate representative from Tark Lonan appeared agitated and worry lines creased his pink forehead.

"Of course, the Clan will do all they can." Cynara paused to study Loring's face. *Does he know the enemy is in his backyard?* "I hope it will be enough. I see Governor Haburn isn't here, Councilman Loring. Is there a reason why he missed this meeting? It is quite unlike him to pass up the opportunity to throw barbs."

"He asked me to convey his regret. Unfortunately, serious problems in the city prevented his attendance today. In fact, he transmitted a message just this morning requesting, if possible, you make a special trip to Tark Lonan."

"For what reason?" Cynara asked. With the issues facing them now, it was an unusual request. "What kind of problems?"

"That he did not say, Princess; however, he asked me to say a meeting with him at Tark Lonan might prove very beneficial to you."

"Very well," she said, making a quick decision. "You may inform Governor Haburn, he can expect me late tomorrow afternoon." Even though she felt something was not as it should be with this request, she knew it would take her personal appearance to reveal Haburn's reasons. He was a peculiar man—bitter, ruthless, and quite enigmatic—and seemingly in bed with an alien. A request from him piqued her curiosity. For now, other matters required attention.

"About the Ama City defenses—and I would advise you to consider these plans for the other cities. Those of you who will take my advice..." She turned to the presentation console to go over the details she had spent the last hour preparing and programming into the city computer. While she couldn't force the city governors to go along, she hoped most of them would put their personal feelings aside and follow these plans.

The city's meager defenses had been severely abused before she assumed office, and they hadn't had time to restore them all to proper working conditions. Although the other cities were in equally poor repair, Ama City was the seat of government, the primary target, and the residence of the power of Arama. With communication links and other vital security equipment in them, her quarters needed protecting. This was why the force field surrounding them was the first to be repaired.

Additional refinements to that defense would improve them, but she didn't mention these while she stressed it was time to ensure all of Ama City's shields were functioning. In this, Rondu could not subjugate her authority. Her plan required a combination of operational defense shields as well as armed guards to protect the power sources.

Civilian guards would be a challenge to recruit, the councilmen argued. The few professional guards were little more than display pieces, elegantly clad men and women employed for formal occasions and special events. Besides, they had no weapons to arm them.

Raising her hands from the table, Cynara nodded agreeably, expecting their objections. "I know, gentlemen. However, if you approach the people with honesty and tell them of my wishes, I feel you will recruit enough guards. Regarding weapons, my quarters include a small arsenal with old but usable weapons..." *Great Tiel, what an understatement.* "...of various types dating back several centuries to the times before the restoration of the Clan of Cantra. These will suffice until we can get in more modern ones from Minos."

"But they were destroyed!" Loring spoke.

"Everyone believed they were destroyed," she explained. "Most of them were, but some—

a few hundred—were saved, preserved, and stored in the royal chambers in case a situation such as this should arise." A brief smile touched her lips. "You see, the Clan was providing aid for us even then." Without waiting for further questions, she explained her plans, pointing out the locations for guards and priority for restoring the active force shields to ensure the best protection of the inner cities.

When she finished, Cynara waited for comments. Her instructions were clear and precise. The councilmen were marginally impressed by them, although none of them could do better. Even if they had been accustomed to thinking in military terms, they wouldn't have been able to manage their resources any better than she had.

"These can be adapted to each city with ease." Her glance went from face to face. "If any of you need my help, I will be available for the next eight hours; however, the computers can calculate most of the necessary changes. I wish to point out—no matter how extensive these plans might seem; our defenses are very meager. We can stop an adversary who expects no defenses at all, but so far as halting an army goes, we can do little more the delay them."

"Then if you are right about alien attackers, we have no hope," Trasarth stated, disbelief showing in his eyes.

"There is always hope. If I am correct, the delay may buy the time we need to study our enemy and find a way to defeat them. The Clan has many resources, as does our settlement on Minos, and they are where our hopes lie. If that's all, I must attend to other business." She slipped out the way she'd come in, not pausing at the invisible spot now. She had her say; it was up to each of the councilmen to make his own decision.

As she marched to her quarters, Cynara wondered why the Clan had allowed the people to grow so dependent on them. Let them grow complacent in a false sense of security. If the Clan had powers to prevent a disaster, she'd seen no evidence of it in the sixteen years she'd lived on Corlan, and she was sure she didn't possess the ability. After a moment, hot tears of frustration dripped down her cheeks, and she shoved anger to the back of her mind. She was part of the Clan's defenses, she reminded herself. Maybe they had more training for her. But it might be too late.

With determination, she punched the control at her waist to deactivate the force field sector covering the entrance to her chambers, stepped through, then turned them on again. A slight buzz and a glowing purplish shimmer were the only indications the field was present. Still, anyone trying to enter would find it solid as a wall and deadly.

Linhok greeted her with an urgent rumbling in his throat and rapid thoughts which took her a minute or two to sort out.

"Are you certain, Linhok?" A dart of her eyes toward the communications console answered her question as clearly as the irritated growl from the frost leopard. A blue pulse filled the corner of the room.

Corlan was calling …

Chapter Seven

UNEXPECTED MEETINGS

THE CITY OF NOCK BAY huddled on the edge of the western coastline like a pig perched awkwardly on a flowerpot. Although open land surrounded it, most buildings centered near the harbor, with homes and smaller businesses clustered within its radius. Two tall towers rose above the other buildings; one featuring an ornate clock that Travis could just make out as he approached. He knew the city market would be near the landmark.

He stopped the wagonner outside the city entrance and debated whether to swing into the city or press on to the next town. He'd been traveling since daybreak, and a hot meal would be welcome. While he had plenty of time to reach Weilock Center, he carried little money, about fifty *tracas* he'd saved up. Still, it wouldn't hurt to visit the city just to say he'd been. With a light heart, he engaged the drive in his vehicle and plunged into the seaside town.

A three-wheeled motorized cart, the wagonner stretched about six feet long and four feet wide at the rear where the flatbed carried his goods. In it, Travis had piled most of his possessions; clothing, a few books, drawing tools, and other assorted items he simply had to have with him, then secured a top over it. At the front, it came to a rounded nose above the primary wheel. While compact, it was not as comfortable as his father's town car and certainly not as fast. But it was easy to find a spot to park, Travis thought when he spotted an opening alongside the road and swung the wagonner into it.

So, this was Nock Bay—a busy city crowded with people conducting business in lines of shops and on corners. To a boy used to small farming towns dotting the countryside, the city looked imposing. He spotted a shop selling sausages in a roll and splurged a little in the market area, even though it was pricier than in Grannar. As he munched the spicy treat, he strolled down to the docks. He'd never been to a port and wasn't sure what to expect, but it certainly wasn't the deep cliff at the road's end, where a steep stairway angled down nearly a hundred feet. Along the smooth beach, several ships were anchored in water barely deep enough for them to float.

As he peered over the edge, he noted watermarks along the cliff, almost to the level where he stood.

"Tide." A youngster, who stopped beside him, supplied.

"What?"

"Tide's out right now," the boy said. "When it's in, it'll come all the way to the upper dock here."

"Oh." Not a witty response, but Travis had little else to say on the subject. He should have thought about it himself, and he felt considerably chagrined to be told by a lad not even as old as Brandon.

"Do you live here in town?" he asked the boy.

"Yeah, most of the time. Sometimes I go out fishin' with my dad. You a farmer?" The kid, used to the bright reflections off the sea, studied him through squinted eyes.

"Actually, I'm a student," Travis answered, pride warming his voice.

"Right," the boy agreed, with a hint of mirth. Then he stared down the street to where a tall man waved at him and muttered, "Gotta go," and ran off.

Travis watched him go, before he turned his gaze back to the harbor. It would be impressive when the tide came in with water lapping at the edges of the upper dock. Sorry he couldn't hang around to see it, Travis sighed and turned back toward the wagonner. He nearly ran into a man about his height who wore black robes and a floppy hood covering his head and face.

"Sorry," he apologized, stepping around him. Peculiar, he thought, to be wearing dark, heavy garments on such a warm day. He didn't recall seeing another outfit like that. Impulsively, he glanced back and saw the figure meet a tall, muscular man who seemed displeased. The tall man made a chopping motion with his hand, then pointed farther down the street, and the two set a quick pace away.

Mildly intrigued, Travis wondered what the meetup was about, but he shrugged it off as none of his business and ambled back up the streets. Eventually, he found his way back to the wagonner. With a last gaze at the city, he pointed the vehicle toward the main gate.

Two hours down the road, he drove through the plains, following the primary route toward the junction, while Nock Bay faded to a small bump behind him. He stopped, gazed appreciatively at the endless blue of the sky and green and yellow crops. It was the first time he'd been beyond his valley, and although the land wasn't much different, it was still fresh territory.

Incredibly, his stomach rumbled, telling him the sausage roll hadn't been enough. With a sigh, Travis ambled to the nearby river, which accompanied him for the last few kilometers, and sank down in the afternoon shade of the tree-lined bank.

He unrolled the food pack his mother had prepared the previous morning and withdrew a chunk of hard, dry bread, which had been fresh and soft at lunch yesterday. A lump of yellow cheese completed his snack. He looked at the food in disgust and muttered, "For an agricultural world, there sure isn't much food around."

"Perhaps you don't know where to look."

Startled, Travis jumped to his feet and peered all around. He hadn't seen anyone, nor did he now, but he'd definitely heard a voice, child-like and feminine. "Where are you? Who are you?"

"Above you. I'm called Zeldana."

Jerking his head up, he scanned the sky and trees for the source but couldn't see anyone. At last, he spotted a large blue and green bird sitting on a thick tree limb, blending in perfectly. He stared in amazement. Of course, he'd heard about kyereagles, but he'd never seen one. In fact, no one he knew ever had. The giant birds never came to the lowlands but kept to their mountain tops. "You're a kyereagle," he stated dumbly.

"Indeed, I am," the bird replied, tilting her head. "And you have my name, but I do not know yours."

"Oh! I'm Travis De … Just Travis." He stammered, still trying to adjust to the talking bird he'd almost believed a myth. The birds not only spoke, but they were an intelligent species.

"Greetings to you, Travis," Zeldana said formally as she fluttered to the ground, nearly tumbling beak-first into the grass.

Instinctively, Travis started to help but stopped when she regained her balance. He realized he wouldn't have known how to help, anyway. "Are you all right?"

"I believe so. I injured my wing two days ago, and it is healing slowly. But it makes flying and landing terribly awkward." She paused, ruffled her feathers, and peered at the dry bread lying on the unrolled clothing. "But, getting back to food, I might help you locate sunberries and other fruit in exchange for a portion of your delicious-looking bread."

Travis cast an unenthused glance at the loaf and shook his head. "I'm afraid it's gotten dried out, but you're welcome to share it with me."

"Then I thank you and suggest you search a little farther along this stream to where it curves slightly toward the mountains. You will find berry vines growing around the trees."

Even though Travis had his doubts, he followed Zeldana's instructions, walking along the river and past the bend. He smiled at the sight of hundreds of sunberry-laden vines growing densely around and through the trees. A few minutes more along the road, and he would have found them himself, he thought as he picked handful after handful to fill his pockets, popping the last few into his mouth. The curious, sweet-yet-tart taste was refreshing, and his spirit climbed again.

When he returned to his wagonner, Zeldana remained as he'd left her, still crouched with her wings tucked tightly against her body. She peered intently at his curious vehicle. He grinned. "There's a whole thicket of wild berries. I suppose you saw them from the air. Well, let's feast while we can." He emptied the berries onto the grass and broke the bread into two pieces.

Together they dined, boy and bird, both silent yet enjoying each other's company. The presence of a human seemed to fascinate the kyereagle as much as the reverse did for Travis. At last, hunger quelled, he leaned back against a tree and asked the question that had lingered throughout the meal. "How did you hurt your wing? You're down low for a kyereagle, aren't you?"

Zeldana lifted her head, and Travis almost interpreted an indecisive expression, although the bird's features couldn't actually convey it. But if she had doubts, she put them aside and answered his question without hesitation. "You're quite right. I am lower than I care to be, and because of this, I injured my wing. I had been flying all night on a reconnaissance trip, so

I was very tired. As I swooped down to search for food, I was nearly assaulted by one of those low-flying mechanical devices. In an attempt to avoid the collision, I clipped a tree. It is a nuisance, and I have been grounded for much longer than I care to be. My kind, as you may be aware, are not at ease in the low meadows."

But Travis's mind was on what she's first said. "Reconnaissance? Why were you flying reconnaissance?"

"Why, don't you know?" Zeldana's voice squawked. "I thought everyone knew."

"What?"

"About poison in the water and Princess Cynara's request for our aid in searching for the criminals who are responsible." Although she pretended to be shocked at his ignorance, Zeldana puffed out her chest, clearly pleased with her knowledge and importance.

Travis realized he would have to pry this information out of her bit by bit. With forced patience, he asked, "What poison? What are you talking about?"

"It's in the river, a terrible poison that's killing the land and even humans. They're poisoning the water, and it is spreading. I am surprised you are not aware of it."

For an intelligent bird, Zeldana struck Travis as scatter-brained. Obviously, she had learned something of importance, but what? He gazed at the cup in his hand. She couldn't mean *this* river water! A dark frown crossed his face. "Listen, Zeldana, I haven't heard any of this. Who is poisoning it? Perhaps you'd better start at the beginning and tell me all you can."

Zeldana plumped out her chest and related her story. "At the Crescent-growing time with the indigo moon high above Sorcerer's Peak, my Lord Randoor, Chieftain of the Kyereagles, held council with Princess Cynara, guardian of Arama. Already my Lord had seen evidence of the disaster of which the princess spoke, and he'd seen the death carried by the waters. Trees and plants lining the bank of the Ama River were dying. The princess begged our help in seeking those responsible, and my Lord Randoor ordered all available kyereagles to search. We are to cover all the land looking for any further evidence of the contamination and seeking any who may appear suspicious. And that, friend Travis, is exactly what I was doing."

Travis absorbed this in silence, his mind reviewing every word. The "crescent-growing time" would have been two nights ago when the moon began to wax. Lord Randoor must be the ruler of the kyereagles, but meeting with Princess Cynara? Did anyone really meet with the sorceress? It seemed unlikely, yet what did he know of government protocol? And death along the Ama River… He recalled the "living pictures" Home Teacher had shown him of the Ama Valley, rich and fertile—even more than his own land—with the silvery Ama River snaking through to supply water to all the fields.

"That would kill all the Ama Valley," he muttered, more to himself than to Zeldana, who watched him curiously.

"That is so," she agreed.

"Did you find anything?"

She shook her head, ruffling the deep blue feathers at her neck. "No. Nothing in this area—yet. It will spread, though; the princess said it would."

"Can she be so sure?"

The bird hopped lightly. "Do you doubt the princess? In matters of this nature, who knows better?"

He felt chastised. Certainly, he wasn't privy to what the sorceress perceived, but he could reason well enough to realize if the poison was spreading, it would eventually reach his parents' farm. Was there anything he could do to help? Most of the water in their valley came from wells which tapped underground rivers. Could the poison contaminate those waters as well?

"Now you see my purpose here. So, may I inquire about yours?"

Uncomprehending, Travis stared blankly at her. After a moment, his mind detached from his own worried thoughts, and he blinked as her words sank in. "My purpose? I'm ..." He hesitated, gazing at the nearby stream before continuing. "I'm going to Weilock Center to study at the university there. Somehow it doesn't seem so important now. I mean, it won't matter much if all the land is destroyed, will it?"

"That I wouldn't know. I'm not acquainted with this university of yours, but it seems a reasonable assumption. Why don't you travel with me, friend Travis? Although I still cannot fly for long, I dare say I might manage short hops to keep up with you. I am bound for the Ama Valley, but we can keep each other company until the fork."

Travis laughed. "I think you might have a problem with that, Zeldana." He pointed to the wagonner. "That's my transportation, and maybe, at full flight, you might keep up with it, but with a damaged wing, I doubt it."

The bird peered hard at the strange three-wheeled contraption and somehow conveyed disappointment.

To be truthful, Travis was reluctant to part from the kyereagle's company. She fascinated him—a sight humans rarely saw— and most of all, she perceived things from a different viewpoint. She would probably provide extraordinary insights into life on Arama. As an idea formed, Travis stared at the waggoner, then at the kyereagle. What did she weigh—about seventy pounds? That shouldn't be a problem.

"I have a plan, Zeldana. I designed my wagonner for hauling things, so you could fit in the back of it. With the top open, we can talk. What do you think?"

Her head craned around, alert bird eyes studying him. Her flat, owlish face seemed to reflect doubt. "I am a little hesitant, friend. Are you sure the thing is safe?"

He grinned, strode next to it, and thumped the plastic shell. "Of course, it is. I've taken it hundreds of places, and I've never had a problem."

Stepping from one taloned foot to the other several times, Zeldana finally agreed. Still, she craned her neck and turned her head to peer at Travis when he lifted her into the back. She squawked in terror when he first started the machine up.

"Let's get going. I'd like to be at Fountain Lake by nightfall," he said cheerfully and engaged the gears.

Zeldana shrieked once more, buried her head under a wing, and kept it there for the next ten minutes. Apparently deciding she would survive this experience, she cautiously straightened her neck and thrust her head back. Travis chuckled at her attempt to recover her dignity.

"This stream empties into the lake. It would be shorter to continue following the river—and less conspicuous," she volunteered.

"That's great, but this machine doesn't fly. It needs a road."

"There is a road," she replied indignantly. "You think I know nothing? It is just a little way up here and to the right. It's a delightful path."

Travis nodded. "Okay, we'll try it."

The path turned out to be exactly that, a dirt way leading across the narrow river then running parallel alongside it. While not as smooth as the main road, the wagonner could manage, so he continued. The drive was beautiful, with tall trees and bushes lining both sides of the stream, and the pleasant sound of water leaping over rocks as it rushed along.

Travis relaxed into the rolling motion of the machine, glanced back at Zeldana, and shouted, "If you'd be willing, I'd like to hear about your mountain home."

Indeed, Zeldana was willing. Within five kilometers, Travis was sorry he'd ever brought the subject up.

As she talked, his mind drifted back to the black-clad person he'd seen in Nock Bay. Travis thought he'd looked suspicious, although the man he spoke to seemed normal. Maybe he should mention it.

Chapter Eight

EXPLORING NEW TERRITORY

THE ORANGE-RED GLOW of sunset tipped the West Ridge Mountains as Travis and Zeldana finally reached their destination. The dirt path wound through a grove of fruit trees, wild and tangled like the berry vines they'd found earlier. They paused to sample the fruit before pressing on. Beyond the woods, the land sloped gently down to the lake.

Barely fifty yards below, the first pool of blue-green water spread into larger basins, linked together like mirrors of the sky. At the center, a geyser spouted a fountain of foamy spray, flecked with pink from the reflected sunset.

Travis gazed in awe. He had seen "living pictures" of Fountain Lake, but nothing prepared him for its scale or beauty. Judging from the fountain's height, he estimated at least four hundred and fifty feet, sometimes higher when bursts surged.

"It's magnificent," he said at last. "What makes it spout like that?"

"How would I know?" Zeldana replied, far less impressed. "I am a kyereagle, not acquainted with aurean things."

"Aurean?" Travis repeated, puzzled.

"Aurean—the dwellers of the low meadows. An ancient Araman word."

He shrugged, watching the sunset mirrored upside-down in the lake. "I wonder if it's poisoned," he murmured.

"Not yet," Zeldana said. "No signs of death here."

Travis nodded, climbed from the wagonner, and knelt at the nearest pool. The water was warm, not icy as he expected. Without hesitation he stripped down, then paused under Zeldana's watchful eyes. Her round gaze flicked from his bare legs to his torso, and he felt suddenly self-conscious. He waded in without fully undressing, the slope dropping quickly until he was swimming.

For fifteen minutes he enjoyed the water, then climbed out, shook himself dry, and dressed. As he buttoned his shirt, he spotted movement in the thicket. Zeldana burst through, waddling fast, feathers fluffed.

"Where have you been? I thought you'd deserted me," Travis said cheerfully.

"Hunting berries around that hill," she answered, pointing with her beak.

"Did you find any?"

"Yes, plenty. But—"

"I could use a snack," he interrupted, already running.

"But I saw two large vehicles—skimmers," she called after him.

He barely heard. Faint engine sounds faded in the distance—more than one, powerful. Strange to see them along this scenic route. Shrugging, he gathered berries, ate a handful, and stuffed the rest into a cloth before returning to the pools. Zeldana waited, agitation plain. They needed to move on.

HOURS LATER, ZELDANA CROUCHED under a tree, feathers ruffled, while Travis muttered beneath the waggoner's hood. The machine had failed just short of the West Ridge entrance. Beyond lay a narrow valley leading to the Sun Mountains, home to Zeldana's bracil—sixty-two kyereagles sheltered in their high eyrie.

With disgust, Travis slammed the cover shut. The drive belt had snapped. Not a major problem—except without a spare in the middle of nowhere. He had tried every trick to rig it, but nothing worked. The next town lay beyond the pass at the joining. With luck, they would have the part.

He glanced at Zeldana, her gaze fixed on the mountains. "Let's see if we can get a ride. You wait here; I'll scout ahead."

Soon a grain transport rumbled toward him. Travis waved, grinning when it halted.

"My waggoner's broken down," he explained. "I need to reach the joining. Can I get a ride?"

"There's room in the back," the driver said.

"Great. Give me a minute." Travis sprinted back, grabbed his food pack and tunic, and called, "Come on, Zeldana."

She hesitated. "Another machine? Another human? I don't think I should. You go on without me."

"Don't be ridiculous," Travis said, unwilling to leave her. "The driver won't even know. It's safe."

Reluctantly, she waddled forward.

"Head to the back. I'll distract him."

The driver shouted impatiently. Travis asked about spare belts, but the man shook his head. "Too long for your toy. Hurry up."

Travis thanked him, hoisted Zeldana into the transport, and vaulted in after her. The vehicle jolted into motion. He leaned against a grain sack, grinning.

"See? I told you it would be fine. Comfortable, too." He closed his eyes, settling in.

Lucky to catch a ride, Travis thought. He had time before Weilock Center. Maybe he should detour to Ama City, see what was happening, and offer aid. Duty to the princess, he told himself. The idea of helping appealed—even if he had no idea how. Like many youths, he carried fantasies of being a hero.

Travis snorted in his sleep, then blinked awake—only to freeze in horror. Zeldana was gleefully scattering kernels from one of the forty-pound grain sacks, spreading them in a golden arc across the floor.

"Oh, noooo," he groaned, crawling over the intervening sacks. "Zeldana, how could you? If the driver sees this, we'll be in real trouble. I can't pay for a sack of grain."

The bird lowered her eyelids, suddenly downcast. "I didn't think he would miss one little sack. I was so hungry, Travis. What will he do?"

"Either turn me over to the authorities or take it out of my hide," Travis muttered, staring at the empty sack. "If we get rid of it, he may not notice until Weilock Center. But you'll have to fly out once he slows near the joining. Head west, parallel the road. I'll get off when he stops."

He scraped the excess grain to the end of the transport, scooping handfuls out onto the road behind them. "Every bird in the valley's getting a feast today, thanks to you," he mumbled.

Zeldana watched mournfully. "I wish I'd eaten more, but I'm too full."

Travis rolled up the empty sack, staring blankly at it. "Looks like I'm definitely going to Ama City with you. This driver's bound for Weilock Center, and I don't dare be anywhere near him when he discovers a whole sack missing."

"I am sorry," Zeldana said softly. "When I'm hungry, I can't help myself."

"Forget it. The damage is done." He shoved the sack beneath the others. "Maybe he'll think he miscounted."

The transport began to slow. Travis glanced sharply at Zeldana. "Quick—get out!" He re-rolled his bundle tightly, disguising the sack. Zeldana scrambled up the highest grain pile, spread her wings, and launched herself with all the grace of an Etorian wild boar. Travis winced as she nearly smashed into the ground, then beat her wings furiously until she rose, transformed into a flowing creature of the sky.

When the transport halted, Travis vaulted down, tapped the cab. "Thanks for the ride."

The driver waved and accelerated away. Travis plunged into the long grass, heart still racing. Minutes later, a dot in the sky grew larger.

Zeldana dove, pulling up barely five feet from a headlong crash.

"That's enough to scare a guy to death!" Travis shouted. "Are you always so reckless?"

"Reckless?" Zeldana puffed her breast. "That was a perfectly controlled maneuver. My wing is still weak, yes, but the rest was exactly as I intended."

"Okay, okay. I believe you," Travis said, though doubts lingered. He turned to survey the valley. They had disembarked between the West Ridge and the Sun Mountains. Ahead lay Marglen, a small town where he hoped to find a new belt. The transport faded northwest, leaving them alone on the road.

"I hope food's as easy to find in the mountains as in the valley," Travis said, thinking of his dwindling supplies.

"Easier," Zeldana assured him. "Small animals, nuts, mountain berries—we'll have no problem."

Travis walked on, thoughts circling. What would he do in Ama City with no food, little money, and only the wagonner? At Weilock Center, he would be cared for—uniforms, quarters, meals. Would Ama City have a place for him?

He thought of his parents' farm, the wells tapping underground rivers. If the poison spread, it would reach them too. His father had always said the soil was their lifeblood. To ignore the danger now felt like betrayal—not just of the Princess, but of his family.

He remembered his mother's eyes when he left—sad, proud, worried. What would she think if he turned away from the threat?

And Cynara… he had seen her once in a living picture, eyes bright with determination. If she was willing to stand against such peril, how could he do less?

Besides, Ama City wasn't so far out of the way. A short detour, he told himself. It wouldn't take much time from his journey to Weilock Center. He could help, even in some small way, and still reach the university.

The thought steadied him. The university would wait. Ama City could not.

The two companions proceeded in silence until they passed the first hills leading into the mountain passage. Marglen was only a little over a mile ahead. If they didn't make it there soon, the few shops in the farming town would close for the day.

While Zeldana had taken flight several times in their trek, she trudged alongside Travis, her gait uneven, showing her exhaustion. "I need to find more food," she said. "I'll take a look around while I'm hunting."

At his nod, the bird took to the sky. He continued onward, glancing up now and then to keep track of Zeldana's progress. She circled a few times around one area, her wings gliding on the air. Abruptly, she shifted to an energetic pumping and made a dive toward the ground. She'd spotted something.

Then, she pulled up abruptly, wings flapping rapidly while climbing, then wheeled around, flying toward him. Travis sensed alarm by her actions and halted, standing still in the middle of the road.

Chapter Nine

A Few Too Many

CYNARA DIRECTED HER SKIMMER to the Ama Valley, electing to go south toward the Elgin River before turning northeast to reach Tark Lonan. In the passenger seat, Linhok sat erect, eyes scanning the terrain as they sped through it.

They'd left Ama City later than she wanted, but with so much going on, she'd had trouble breaking away. Investigations into the wall's bombing hadn't revealed anything conclusive; no indication of who set them. Then she'd spent more time on three separate calls to Corlan, bringing the Clan up to speed. They were skeptical of her report of alien beings, suggesting they were simply a race she hadn't encountered before, although they couldn't identify them. Likewise, her mentor felt the bombs were from a band of disgruntled citizens and nothing concerning.

Shuranil didn't believe you. Linhok's mental voice pulled her out of her reverie.

"No, he didn't. Like everyone else, Corlan isn't taking the threat seriously. Not until I can get proof." She glanced at the serene-looking white animal. He'd insisted on coming with her to Tark Lonan today.

The incidents happened too closely together. You do not trust Haburn, so I wish to protect you.

He could be right. She'd seen a foreign-looking man there, and he wasn't simply some race she hadn't encountered on an Araman planet. "I'm glad you came."

Why did you choose to go this route?

"I wanted to see the Elgin River. If it's been affected by the red algae yet. If the invaders only poisoned the Dangon River, I can get an indication of how fast it's spreading. Since the Dangon flows north and into the sea through the Tang, the algae might not infect the Sila or Elgin. Whoever did it doesn't understand how the waters flow here."

Maybe the intent is not to poison the land but to create panic.

"All they have to do is show themselves to achieve that goal." She figured if the Aramans saw them, they'd come running to her for protection. What could she do against an invasion? Her gifts weren't powerful enough to hold off an army. She wasn't sure their shields could either. And Corlan? Did the Clan have anything capable of a strong defense?

Ahead, she saw the river shining like a silver band through the green and gold farmlands. Around her skimmer, the crops looked plentiful and healthy, suggesting Elgin's waters were contaminant-free and providing plenty of irrigation water. Drainage from the West Ridge and Sun Mountains fed various streams leading to the Elgin and the Sila, which merged one hundred and ten kilometers from Ama City. A deep breath of relief slipped out.

She continued to the river and flew over it to the east until she passed the merge with the Sila River. Both looked clean and flowing well. Satisfied they weren't in danger, she turned north, up the valley toward the Sun Mountains.

Not far from the rising hills and bluffs that marked the range, Cynara took the turnoff to Tark Lonan, following the road to skirt around the giant peaks ahead. This part of the valley road provided spectacular views filled with trees and berry bushes. Come fall, they would be a glorious palette of colors, a feast for the eyes and the soul. She smiled, savoring the pastoral scene.

Then, the buzz of an engine noise grew, accompanied by another. She glanced at the rearview monitor, seeing a pair of skimmers racing behind her. They looked like messenger-class models with dark blue bodies and silver tops, two-seaters and fast. "I have a feeling those skimmers are not good news, Linhok. Hang on. I'll try to evade them. If they're harmless, they won't stick with me."

Linhok crouched low, paws curled around the seat. Cynara veered toward the foothills, where bushes and stone outcroppings offered cover. Should this be an attack, she didn't want to get caught in the middle of the clear route. Dismayed, she saw the first skimmer track her turn, then the second followed. Worse, she glimpsed a third one farther back.

She turned her vehicle to parallel the hills, focusing her thoughts on stopping the skimmers behind her. Her magic was elemental; simple things like reducing the air to the engines could cause them to stall. She whispered her power words, pulling the air toward her. One skimmer sputtered and lost momentum, slowing to fall behind the others. She glimpsed back to pick the next target when Linhok's growl snapped her attention forward. A new vehicle barreled straight at her.

Where did it come from?

Woods to the right, my lady, Linhok warned.

She veered to avoid it, but the vehicle clipped her skimmer, sending it skidding toward a boulder. Though she fought to control it, the unit crunched the backend into a tree trunk before it ricocheted, skidding across the open ground. Cynara attempted to restart the engine, got no response, and frantically looked around. Two pursuers landed. Black-clad figures climbed out, faces covered by helmets. The skimmer that had caught her head-on circled around and landed on the ground nearby.

"Run!" She threw the hood open, climbed out, and sprinted toward the rock and bush-covered hills where she could hide yet gain a good view. Looking back, she saw Linhok leap out, pausing to stare at their pursuers as they chased after her. He launched himself at the closest pair, who responded by veering to their right and running for the woods. Linhok pursued. The other two continued toward her.

Cynara went for the high ground, scrambling uphill and diving into the bushes to mask her progress. Circling left, she found a niche behind a rocky shelf jutting out of the dirt. She peered over the edge, seeing a taller figure exit from the skimmer that had rammed her. He joined the other two, meeting them midway. Good. They were close together. She drew a deep breath and concentrated on her next spell. Whispering under her breath, she envisioned the form it would take and thrust her right hand forward, fingers spread wide.

A burst of white light exploded in front of the trio coming toward her. When it faded, the victims thrashed about, bending over. They clawed at their helmet visors, rubbing at their eyes. One dropped to his knees, hands covering his face. The taller one wiped his face with a cloth, then looked toward her. Had he gauged her location from that? How?

A scream came from the trees, followed by a shriek of pain. Linhok had found his target. She shuddered, knowing what the leopard could do to its prey. By now, the other man would be fleeing in a panic. Linhok would find him.

She shifted her attention to the now recovering taller man uphill from her and spotted the last skimmer—the one she had temporarily disabled—landing nearby. Two more black-clad men climbed out.

Cynara's heart lurched. Eight? Someone had sent eight after her? Why? Her training didn't include hand-to-hand combat, most of it fine-tuning her magical skills, not real fighting.

One pointed toward her, pulled out a long weapon and knelt, hefting it to his shoulder.

But she could move objects and cast illusions. She focused, lifted a nearby stone the size of an orange, and directed it toward the kneeling person with all her strength. It shot across the distance faster than the shooter could get his weapon positioned. Spotting the moving object, the other one dove toward his companion, too late. The rock smashed into the shooter's head just as he fired a laser beam and his hand jerked before the projectile hit his head, knocking him out. The other one leaped back, turned, and ran behind the skimmer as Cynara hurled another two stones toward them.

She swung around to face her above attacker and gasped. He wasn't in sight. She scanned the hillside for any movement but spotted nothing. He'd slipped away while the others distracted her.

Across the way, the ping of a laser weapon cut through the air, and Cynara caught her breath. *Linhok?* No answer. She feared her companion had been shot. Was he injured or dead? Then, another shriek pierced the air. Linhok destroyed his other prey.

Safe. Coming to your aid.

Turning toward the recent skimmer, she saw the two hunters were on their feet and racing toward her on foot. Focusing, Cynara cast an illusion. The ground split open, making a ravine deep enough to swallow a man. They stumbled, halting just short of it, and backed up. The spell would last only a few minutes, but it bought her time.

She scrambled down to another rocky position lower down. Once settled, she cast her gaze to the men behind the illusion in time to see

Linhok charge from the woods and sprint toward the nearest person.

At first, the victim didn't see the big cat but Linhok's pounding paws alerted him and he spun toward the fast-approaching cat. Shaken, he yanked his weapon out, fumbling as he tried to take aim. Too slow. The cat was on him a moment before he could fire it, and Linhok's claws raked down his front. A scream erupted as blood splattered over the white cat, adding to the streaks already on his fur.

The other one retreated, his hand reaching for a weapon. Cynara teleported a log into his path and he stumbled over it, falling to his knees. She readied another stone, reaching out for it mentally when a hand clamped down on her wrist. A strong arm locked around her shoulder. She twisted, struggling to break free. Summoning a broken branch, she clubbed him hard in the shoulder. He didn't let go.

"Don't fight me," he growled. "Come quietly, and you won't get hurt."

She closed her eyes tightly, blasting dirt-laden wind into his face. His hands flew to his eyes. Seizing the moment, she leaped, rolling down the hillside, crashing through brush and over stones. Above her, she heard an eagle shriek. She glimpsed it in the sky just before her head slammed into a boulder.

Chapter Ten

A Few Feathers Lost

ZELDANA SWOOPED LOW AND shouted at Travis. "Trouble ahead—toward the mountains. Hurry!" Then she beat her wings hard, soaring back the way she'd come.

Travis ran, shoving branches and bushes aside until he emerged into the clearing, his feet skidding when he pulled to a halt. Ahead, a huge, white, blood-splattered feline paired off with a black-clad person, who circled the beast, brandishing a long knife weapon. A trio of mauled bodies littered the clearing.

Travis' eyes tracked beyond, to where Zeldana circled above a troublesome scene. Similarly clothed to the other man, a tall figure emerged from the trees at the base of a hill and strode toward the rocky outcropping where a female body sprawled, unmoving across the rocks. As the kyereagle dove toward the ground, he sprinted toward them.

Zeldana skimmed low, flying barely a meter above their heads. The man ducked his head, partially crouching. As the bird zipped away, his head followed her. Travis faltered, unsure why he was here or what he could possibly do.

"Help the girl!" Zeldana shrieked at him when she swooped past again. Then she altered her course and plummeted toward the other masked attacker doing battle with the white cat. Travis watched long enough to see her divert the man's attention. Clearly, she deemed the guys in black to be the villains while the girl and the big feline were the victims.

He dove into the distracted man ahead of him and shoved the attacker aside by throwing his full weight against him. The bigger and stronger man soon retaliated, throwing punches at Travis. He wasn't a trained fighter, but his farm-honed agility allowed him to dodge several blows, landing a few of his own. Just when his confidence rose, a brutal uppercut snapped his jaw sideways and sent him sprawling.

From the other battle, Travis heard a scream along with the snarls and growls of the big cat. Overhead, shrill bird calls from Zeldana accompanied whatever fight occurred there. Shaking his head clear, Travis glimpsed the white beast's spring, claws flashing, as it brought the man down in a final, savage strike. He shuddered involuntarily but turned his attention back to his own battle.

The man he'd been fighting had turned to watch the other battle. With the final scream from his cohort, he stiffened. Travis looked back to see the white cat racing toward them. When he turned back to his opponent, the man moved toward the young woman, who lay motionless on the ground, oblivious to them.

Travis clambered to his feet and prepared to throw himself at the man again.

The attacker knelt by his quarry, taking a moment to peer at her. When the man moved to lift the unconscious girl, Travis leaped for him. His body collided into the bigger person, knocking him off balance. The impact sent both tumbling away from the woman.

The assailant was on his feet while Travis still lay prone and gasping for breath, but he didn't waste any more time. Travis watched as he spun around and broke into a run toward his skimmer as the big cat closed in. Even though the feline moved fast, the man's lead was just enough to reach the skimmer and activate it before the animal could intercept him. All the while, Zeldana circled overhead, shrieking and urging them on.

The skimmer bucked wildly under the driver's frantic hands, rearing like an unruly stallion before lurching sideways. With the cat nearly on the skimmer, the driver plunged it to the right, banging into another blue vehicle, then finally found the elevate control. The car shot up over two meters, almost colliding with Zeldana, who'd swung low. A few feathers from the ruffled kyereagle fluttered to the ground, and the skimmer shot forward, moving away from them.

Groaning, Travis crawled to his knees, clutching at his stomach, as he fought to breathe. He didn't have another round with the ruffian in him, so he was grateful he'd cut his losses and run.

With the initial target vanished, the cat stalked back toward him and the woman. Eyeing the bloodstains from its previous fight, Travis scooted back away from the fallen girl.

Zeldana circled once, then settled on one of the large boulders, dancing from foot to foot. Keeping a wary eye on the silently approaching white and red apparition of death personified, she asked, "Are you all right?"

He nodded, wet his dry lips, and finally found his voice. "I'm okay. Are you?"

"A few feathers lost is all." She fluttered her wings anxiously. "I hope this creature isn't hungry, though."

Travis turned his gaze to the approaching cat. If anything, the animal seemed exhausted. Even with the blood-spattered coat, he could admire the beauty and strength of this incredible beast, but, like Zeldana, he confessed to being fearful. However, the feline seemed indifferent to them; its attention riveted on the inert form of the young woman.

Travis's eyes followed the fixed gaze of the cat and stopped once they came upon the unmoving girl. Huge cat forgotten, he forced himself to his feet and staggered over to kneel beside her. Long dark lashes lay motionless against her cheeks, and silky platinum strands of hair curled loosely around her face and shoulders.

For a heartbeat, Travis stared at her beauty, until his gaze fell on her purple and blue bruised and twisted hand, fingers bent unnaturally. He noticed the sharply pointed vinte grasped tightly in her left hand. He turned toward Zeldana. "She's been hurt. Would you get my bundle? There's some water in it." He glanced down at his timeband and tried to estimate how long it would take to get the injured girl into Marglen. He worried they might not have enough time.

As he turned back to her, he glimpsed white movement out of the corner of his eye and held his breath. The cat approached within four feet before it halted, its unblinking gaze focused on Travis. He exhaled slowly. Rocking back on his heels, every muscle taut, ready to bolt if the animal came closer.

After several moments, during which Travis felt his life slipping away with clear visions of the dead man flashing through his mind, the cat stretched out on the ground, tucked his front paws in, and brought his tail around in apparent satisfaction to wait and watch. With considerable effort, Travis relaxed, forced his heartbeat to slow, and breathed deeply. He moved toward the girl again, a cautious hand reaching toward the vinte in her left hand.

His fingers were almost on it, ready to grasp, when the cat snarled and tensed. Jerking his hand back, Travis jumped a good three feet away and froze, staring at the animal. He forced himself to speak, not expecting the animal to understand but hoping his voice sounded reassuring. "It's okay. I'm not going to hurt her—or you. I want to help. It will be okay. Trust me."

Zeldana came to an uncertain landing behind Travis. With his attention still locked on the white cat, he asked, "Do you think he's going to attack?"

She dropped the bundle, peeked over Travis's shoulder, and replied, "I don't believe so. Not at the moment, anyway. See, his muscles aren't tensed, and his paws aren't positioned for a strike."

Travis nodded, reached back for the bundle, and fumbled to remove the small flask secured in the middle. His numb fingers tugged until the parcel separated into clothing and bag, freeing the flask. He was ready to take the first sip himself, then a soft moan from the girl demanded his attention. The cat was forgotten and he moved to her.

Carefully, he eased his arm around her shoulder and lifted her so she could lean against him. He tried not to jar her right hand but winced with her when she cried out in pain as it struck a small rock.

"I'm sorry! I—" He broke off, staring as her deep blue eyes opened wide and her lips parted in a whimper. He had never seen eyes like that—turquoise saucers, rich and deep, unlike the faded blue-gray or browns of most Aramans. She bit down on her lip as she tried to move her hand. She squeezed her eyes shut and a tear slipped from one corner.

Gently, Travis reached for her right wrist and lifted the injured hand, setting it safely in her lap. She slumped against him, and he thought she'd passed out again, but she forced her eyes open once more. He grabbed the flask of water and offered it to her.

"It's only water," he apologized. "I wish it were something stronger."

She sipped slowly, seeming to become aware of him. As her eyes lowered, so did his, following down her other arm to where her good hand clutched the vinte. The blade's point now rested against Travis' thigh. With effort, her fingers relaxed, letting the weapon drop into the dirt.

Her expression looked distant, and Travis worried she was going to pass out again. After several moments, she turned her gaze to him, studying his features, then looked beyond him to the oversized bird. She cleared her throat. “My companion and I appear to be indebted to you for our lives. To whom do we owe our gratitude?"

Travis flushed. Her voice was as beautiful as she was, her speech more proper than the folks back home. "I'm Travis DeLonghe. My friend is Zeldana, a kyereagle from the Sun Mountains."

She nodded briefly in acknowledgment, a flicker of interest crossing her face at the mention of Zeldana. She pressed against Travis as she attempted to get to her feet, and the boy slid his arm around her waist to assist. Pressing her lips together, she pulled herself up, grunting at the pain. Travis stared in amazement to discover she was nearly as tall as he, her head a mere two inches below his.

She looked past him to see Zeldana. The bird still huddled warily, ready to take flight if necessary. The girl appeared to notice Zeldana’s discomfort. In a gentle voice, she said, "Do not fear Linhok. He is an intelligent frost leopard from Polara. I assure you he will not harm you. An honor to meet you, Zeldana, *mijia kyeria*. I know the leader of your bracil."

Startled at the hearing the familiar terms in the ancient language of her people, Zeldana jerked her head sharply toward the girl and peered more closely. She dipped her head in a formal salute. "I serve where I can if you are, in truth, Princess—"

"I am Cynara," she interrupted, "Princess of Arama."

It took a moment for Travis to realize what she'd said, then his face paled. "My Lady! I—I'm sorry. I didn't know." Frantically, he worried, what was the penalty for touching a royal sorceress?

Unexpectedly, she laughed. "Sorry for what? For helping me?" Then her face grew serious. "Siri DeLonghe, are you all right?"

Travis sank slowly onto a boulder. "I think so. Who—" He swallowed nervously and dipped his head toward the mutilated corpse. "—were your attackers?"

Cynara followed his look and stared coldly at the body. "An excellent question—and I think it's time to have a closer look at that one."

As they moved toward the corpse, Travis caught a faint glimmer on the attacker's hand. The skin looked wrong, etched with dark lines that pulsed faintly, as if alive. It wasn't anything he had ever seen on an Araman. A chill ran through him. Whatever this was, it wasn't natural.

Travis gulped, not sure he had the stomach for it but continued with her. For all her strength, the Princess seemed weakened and grabbed his arm for support.

formal salute?" Sorry, where I [illegible] if you are, in truth, Princess—"

"I am Cynara," she interrupted. "Princess of Arcana."

It took a moment for Travis to realize what she'd said, then his face paled. "My Lady! I—I'm sorry, I didn't know." Frantically, he wondered, what was the penalty for touching a royal sorceress?

Unexpectedly, she laughed. "Sorry for what? For helping me?" Then her face grew solemn. "Sir DeLongpre, are you all right?"

Travis sank slowly onto a boulder. "I think so. What—" He swallowed nervously and sloped his head toward the mutilated corpse. "—were your attackers?"

Cynara followed his look and stared coldly at the body. "An excellent question—and I think it's time to have a closer look at that one."

As they moved toward the corpse, Travis caught a faint glimmer on the attacker's head. The skin looked wrong, etched with dark lines that pulsed faintly as if alive. It wasn't anything he had ever seen on an Arcanan. A chill ran through him. Whatever this was, it wasn't natural.

Travis gulped, not sure he had the stomach for it, but continued with her. For all her strength, the Princess seemed weakened and grabbed his arm for support.

Chapter Eleven

Not of This World

HIGH SHARP-PLANED CHEEKS, angular jowl, eyes so black they appeared pupilless, and skin of amber—all alien. Totally, completely alien.

Still holding the black mask, Cynara studied the lifeless figure. Across from her, Travis gaped at the corpse, his jaw dropped and eyes wide with shock.

"What is it?" he muttered.

"An alien being," Cynara replied. "One not of this solar system."

So, you were right, Linhok's mind said quickly.

I was right. It was a sad agreement.

Travis stared at Cynara. "You mean this—this being—is from another star system? But how? What's *it* doing here?"

She turned her eyes toward Travis, her eyebrows lifting a touch in surprise. "You understand life can come from another system? That it's not limited to this star system? You're not surprised?"

"Surprised? Yes. At least, to find an alien here, but not surprised another star supports life. That's only logical."

He sounded so matter of fact about it that Cynara almost laughed. "Do you realize there are a number of people on the High Council who find it ludicrous? In fact, I don't think any—"

"It has happened at last," Zeldana said abruptly, her voice filled with awe.

Until then, she'd been so quiet Cynara barely noticed her watching. Both Travis and Cynara turned to stare at the eagle, but she voiced the question. "What do you mean? What do you know about this?"

Zeldana hopped at the sharpness in her voice. "N-n-nothing, your Highness. I don't know anything! Just what's in the Souuifan."

"I'm sorry, Zeldana. I didn't mean to snap at you. Tell me, what is this about the Souuifan? I don't recall it mentioning anything of this sort."

"It is only in the original lore, not in the translations. It's not much, really." Zeldana paused as if afraid to speak.

"Go on," Cynara prodded gently.

The bird took a stance, puffing her feathers up and thrusting her chest out. In her sing-song voice, she began to recite the lore. "At the zenith of the double moons in the year of Tiel's grace, the High Council of the Clan of Cantra held a gathering, and all were represented. Lord Galancoor of the Glass Bracil stood for all Eagles and went in peace alongside hunted and hunter alike. There was great feasting and merriment until just before the first light of Astara when King Asayian rose in a state of *ecorin* to speak. And he spoke thusly:

'For our world and her sisters of the father Astara, I see events of great import and long sequences of time. Strangers will come twice to the world of flowers and sun, one offering friendship, one bringing *okian*. Thousands of cycles of Astara will separate these events, and many changes will be wrought between the two.'

So spoke King Asayian, and none doubted the truth, but few understood. Lord Galancoor brought the message to the Eagles, and it was duly recorded."

An uneasy silence followed Zeldana's recitation. Princess Cynara shivered despite herself. This legend of the kyereagles was like the myth she'd read as a child on Corlan, the one she was told to forget as baseless. Yet here lay proof before her eyes.

"What's *okian*? Did I hear the word right?" Travis asked. "I thought I understood most of that, but there were a few words … " He looked toward Cynara.

"Death," Cynara replied flatly. "King Asayian ruled the planets over a thousand years ago. At the time of this prediction, he was two hundred and twelve years old. Many thought his *ecorin*—that's the trance-like state brought on using sunberries and *tarlac* leaves mixed together—to be deteriorating, and the things he said were false. They did not take his predictions, especially this one, seriously. It was recorded, as required, but annotated as questionable. Just as it was omitted from the Souuifan, so it was omitted from the books of the Clan of Cantra."

"Was King Asayian referring to this—" He looked once again at the alien face. "—being as one of the strangers? And if this one is bringing death, what about the one offering friendship?"

With a shrug, Cynara knelt to cover the face of the alien man with the mask again. "Who knows? Perhaps King Asayian was delirious in his ecorin, and only part is true. This alien is not too different from us. Hard, sharp cheekbones lengthen his face. A slightly smaller race, constructed basically the same as our people. And his flesh turns cold at death, like ours." She straightened, brushing off her hands as if touching the dead had contaminated her.

Yet the prophecy lingered in her mind. *Strangers will come twice.* If this one brought death, then another must still come—and perhaps that one held the key to survival.

Travis shifted his eyes to the other dead bodies littering the ground. "What should we do with the bodies?"

"They deserve a decent burial. Even an alien. Linhok?"

It is so, my Lady. Linhok rose, surveyed the area. *By the riji tree near your skimmer, perhaps?*

"It's a good location. I'll help." She straightened, took a step toward the squatty umbrella-shaped tree.

No. I killed him. I will dig alone.

"Very well, Linhok. It's your choice."

Travis stared hard at her. "Are you talking to the leopard?"

"Yes—in a way. Linhok and I communicate telepathically, although I sometimes say what I'm thinking out loud. He understands them, but the thoughts are clearer."

"There's a difference?"

"Oh, yes. When we think, it's in symbols and images, not words. Symbols are universal, understood by any intelligent life where words fail. Usually, when I hear messages from Linhok, my mind converts them into words and complete phrases. I'm not sure how his mind handles my thoughts."

Nodding, Travis gazed to where the frost leopard had begun digging in the soft earth a few feet from the riji tree. "I definitely underestimated Linhok," he murmured softly.

"Many people do." Pain and exhaustion from her fight caught up with Cynara, and she suddenly sagged. Travis reached to steady her.

Through her aches and private sorrows, Cynara smiled at him. "No longer afraid of me?"

Travis' face reddened a shade, and he shook his head.

"Good," she continued. "For I need your services if you're willing to give them."

"Anything, my Lady."

She flashed a brief smile. "You speak quickly, Travis. Not even a moment to consider what you might be getting into?" She suddenly swayed, her knees weak. Her voice wavered as dizziness struck. Her head throbbed, and she suspected a mild concussion.

Travis glanced around, spotting a toppled tree shaded by the foliage of another. He urged the Princess toward it, helped her ease her strained body down on it. Seeing his look of concern, she waved it away.

"It's nothing. I'll be all right in a few minutes." Her swelling left hand suggested otherwise, but she kept the thought to herself. For now, she had questions to be answered before she trusted this young man any further.

"Are you sure, my Lady?" Travis asked, his voice sounding worried. "There's a small town near here, and we might be able to find help there."

She shook her head, long hair swinging across her face like a veil. "No, I would prefer not to go into town. There was trouble here, and I would rather not draw attention to myself."

She shifted her gaze to where Linhok still dug busily, his powerful forelegs rapidly widening the hole he'd begun, then looked back to Travis. He stood beside her, but his eyes had followed hers to the frost leopard. She studied him carefully—a youth, slightly taller than she, slender but bronzed and muscled from fieldwork. His breeches and tunic were of good quality, suggesting his family did well. A bruise darkened his jaw, his cheeks were dust-streaked, but his blue-gray eyes were clear and readable.

"I would like to know," she said, "what a farm boy is doing in the Sun Mountains and how he comes to be in the company of a kyereagle?"

Travis' eyes slid back to her, and he answered simply. "Well, I was on my way to the University at Weilock Center, but I met Zeldana, and we decided to go to Ama City together." He grinned sheepishly and began telling her the whole story, omitting no details. When he told her about the pilfered bag of grain, Cynara laughed merrily, her low, melodious sound making him smile in return.

Cynara turned her gaze to where the source of their merriment busily examined one of the blue and white skimmers. She circled it a third time, then shrieked suddenly, the sound sharp and incomprehensible.

Travis's laughter cut off, and Linhok's head bobbed up from his digging as they all stared in surprise at the excited bird. She fluttered her wings uncontrollably.

"She might be in trouble," Travis said, and he ran toward her.

Cynara followed behind him at a slower pace, but close enough to hear when he called out to the kyereagle.

"Zeldana! What—?"

"It's one of them!" she shouted. "I should have recognized it sooner. How could I be so dumb?" Although calmer now, she still craned her neck back and forth.

"What are you talking about?"

"I didn't tell you about it last night, but I saw this skimmer just yesterday—or at least, one like it. Remember when we were at Fountain Lake, and you'd gone into the pool, and I'd gone looking for berries? That's when I saw them. They went past me. I only glimpsed them, but I'm sure this is one. I think it's also like the one that injured my wing. I recognized the sound it made."

Cynara joined them and studied the skimmer intently. Images flashed in her mind, her pupils dilating as she slipped into a near-trance. In slow motion, her hand—the injured one, at that—reached out. Her fingers touched the surface, pressed against it in an almost caressing motion. Abruptly, she cried out in shock and pain, collapsing like a ragdoll to the ground.

Chapter Twelve

An Unplanned Excursion

CYNARA MOVED BETWEEN DARKNESS and a kaleidoscope of light. Colors flashed and whirled, then receded to let black flood in again. White scenes flickered against the void—stark, unreal, alien. She was part, but not a part, of the fantastic array of impressions around her.

She knew she was traveling, but it was unlike anything she'd experienced before. Not her world, not any place she knew, and she had no idea how she'd arrived. First, all was a void, then it sparked with intense color, and she couldn't hide her eyes from it. She had no control, barely even the ability to reason.

Something—or someone—touched her, tried to call her back, but she couldn't respond. She moved into inkiness again; a void filled with bursting flashes of light. A galaxy of stars flowed into a spiral. Or was she inside the swirl itself? She moved through emptiness toward one bright point. It flashed and sparkled, flowing brilliantly. As she drew closer, she saw an anemic-looking yellow orb, yet its radiance was as intense as Astara. At least a dozen smaller globes formed lop-sided rings around it.

Abruptly one of the globes leaped toward her, a sphere of blood-red marbled with gold. As her view focused, she saw the details of the stark burning world. Deep red sand shifted endlessly, violent winds painting it like a mad artist's brush. An endless desert stretched before her, broken only by rough golden mountains strong enough to resist the waves of sand and wind. Sheltered valleys held fortress-like cities, angular towers built from the red stone itself.

Cynara's vision reeled, whirling almost like the wind as she swept past tower after tower. She was unable to analyze, only to see, feel, and record. Her mind cataloged everything—the heat, the dryness, the burning colors, the exotic design. Then she saw the flash of a skimmer, much like the one she'd touched to trigger this vision. It crossed the sands toward a gate of red stone and shiny metal. Beyond the gate was an area filled with thousands of beings in black and gray garb, all with the same alien features as the dead one on Arama.

She rose higher, her vision showing a flat rooftop with hundreds of shiny black oblong spaceships parked. Gray-clad figures swarmed around them, readying them for use. An invasion armada. Her mind connected the impression with sudden clarity.

Abruptly, she was flung away, whirled back through the star spiral and into blackness again.

She floated in darkness for a long time. No sense of time or space—only suspension, numb and uncaring.

After a while, Cynara stood at the edge of cleft in a mountain face surrounded by trees, where the embankment dropped to the valley below. A figure huddled near a warming fire and a kyereagle nearby. Although she felt she should recognize them, she did not—only sensed familiarity. Next to the huddling body was a large bundle wrapped in cloth. She moved toward it until she realized the bundle was her own body. She'd returned at last.

Uncertain of re-entry for the first time since childhood, she stood next to her inert form and stared. Something touched her mind, probing slightly, like a whisper of breeze through grain. She wasn't afraid; she drew comfort and encouragement from it. Detecting the source, she turned to see the ghostly cat emerging from the forest. He carried a small animal in his mouth, but his ears flicked forward.

Rotating, she caught the concerned look on the young man's face as he watched her unmoving shell for any sign of life. Linhok dropped his catch at the youth's feet and stretched out beside her to wait. He knew she was back, and suddenly, it was easy.

She saw Travis reach for the dead alphare and snap the furry creature up. Worry haunted his eyes, his mouth set in a grim line.

She moaned, the soft sound barely audible. Linhok's ears flicked, and a slow rumble of affection began. Like a kitten, the big cat pushed his head against her fingers, rubbing back and forth. She responded, slipping back into her body.

The throbbing in her injured hand brought Cynara back to consciousness quicker than usual. Her eyes popped open, gaze falling on her bulkily bandaged hand. She frowned and began to push herself up.

Startled, Travis jumped and went to her. "Are you all right? We were worried." He slid his arm around her shoulders to help.

She tried to nod, but her head dipped only slightly. Her voice rasped. "I'm okay. Is there any water?"

He still supported her shoulders while he stretched to reach the flask. "I wasn't sure what to do, so I brought you here. We hid the skimmers. I thought maybe in the morning—"

"It's all right," she interrupted, too weary to listen further. She placed her good hand on his arm in reassurance. "I'm sure you did everything you could."

He leaned back, observing as she drank. She watched his eyes, seeing the concern in them. Finally, he asked, "Is there anything I can do, my Lady?"

For a long moment, she gazed into his eyes, then decided. "Yes, there are three things you can do for me. First, if you are to be my friend, you can start by calling me Cynara. Second, I would appreciate your help in getting to that boulder, so I may lean against it. And third, if you know how to skin and cook the alphare, I wish you'd do it. I'm famished."

With a grin, Travis hastened to comply. Once she was settled comfortably with the cloak around her, he turned to prepare the alphare.

WHILE HE SKINNED THE plump animal, Travis explained that earlier, when Cynara collapsed, he and Linhok had carried her away from the skimmer site. They found this sheltered clearing tucked beneath the trees, hidden from the open ground where the fighting had occurred. He'd built a small fire there, and Zeldana perched high above to keep watch. It wasn't far, but it was safer, concealed from any hunting party that might return.

Cynara watched him, fascinated by the preparations. She knew nothing about cooking; her meals had always been prepared for her. It had never seemed necessary. Neither had the martial use of the vinte seemed necessary, she reflected, yet she'd pressed to learn the art even when the Clan lords argued against it. A fine lot of good it did today.

While the alphare cooked, she forced herself to think about her strange experience. At first, Linhok tried to follow her thoughts but soon found them incomprehensible. *I'm not sure if I fully understand*, she told him mentally, *but I think it explains a lot. Perhaps when I tell Travis, the remainder will sort itself out.*

Tell the boy? Is it wise?

We must trust him, Linhok. He should know what it is we face.

Nonetheless, she didn't say anything until after they had eaten. Zeldana located a secure perch in a nearby tree to keep watch. Cynara watched Travis dump another log on the fire and caught the quick glances he made her way. He walked back and settled himself at her side. "Is something wrong?"

"In a way, but it's difficult to explain." Uncertain how to begin, she focused her gaze on the warming blaze and tried to organize her thoughts. How much would this boy understand?

"Does it have something to do with what happened when you touched the skimmer? Where were you?"

She turned her head toward him, and her jaw dropped. "Do you understand what was happening?"

"Not completely," he answered, "only that even if your body was here, you were not really with it. You were unconscious, but it was abnormal—no sounds or small movements. It was like you were frozen or suspended. Not dead, but not here."

"You are quite perceptive," she stated in appreciation. She would have to learn not to underestimate him. "Travis, I was traveling in astral form. Do you know what it is?"

He shook his head.

"It's the soul leaving one's physical body. Once separated, with the outer shell left in suspension, as you so aptly put it, the astral or spirit body can travel freely. Apparently, touching the surface of the vehicle provided an instant stimulus to create this separation.

"To be honest, I've never done it like that. I usually have trouble with leaving my body. This was like being hurtled through time and space, not fully conscious of what was happening, yet seeing fragments as I went. Then I was viewing another planet—bleak, barren. A desert world, I think. It rotated around a pale-yellow star, smaller than Astara yet very bright and hot. It's the aliens' home world. I saw thousands of beings like him, dressed as he was."

Travis shuddered visibly, his shoulders shaking. He wet his lips and asked, "Thousands more like him? Do you suppose they're coming here, too"

She shrugged. " I don't know. I saw only one city. They must have hundreds on the planet. Possibly, thousands. I don't know, but I suspect they will if we don't stop them."

"Then what you saw was probably related to the skimmer. The skin material isn't like ours. It's more porous than anything we use. Touching it must have linked you to the alien world somehow."

"Of course! It's similar to when I touch objects and see past events and people from them--except those times aren't so violent. Perhaps it's the alien metal..."

"Or maybe it's a combination of both," Travis said, his eyes growing wider. "The touch may have keyed some impressions which in turn triggered one of these astral journeys. Is it possible?"

"Yes, it's possible," Cynara answered slowly. "It's never happened before—at least, not to me, but I suppose it could." She gazed at him, reassessing this farm boy. "Has it happened to you?"

"Me?" Travis squeaked, eyes popping. "In Tiel's name, no! This is the first time I've even heard of it. What made you even think that?"

She dipped her face, feeling a warm blush touch her cheeks. "It's just... Well, you seem so familiar with the concept—like you knew."

"It seemed logical, that's all." He rubbed his shoulders as if chilled and reached for another stick of wood to toss onto the fire.

SILENCE FOLLOWED, EACH LOST in private thoughts. Double shadows filled the forest as the moon edged over a peak to join Corlan's glowing circle. A haze filtered the atmosphere, silver halos encircling both globes.

Cynara's thoughts turned to her world—the one she called home. She wondered what was happening there, and if anyone would track the aliens when they came. And they were coming. She'd seen the invasion fleet. Yet the Clan hadn't believed her warnings. With time running out, she knew they couldn't linger here. Even concealed, another hunting party could stumble upon them. They needed to relocate quickly and return to Ama City.

Clearing his throat, Travis asked, *"What's it like?"*

Eyes half-closed, she turned. *"What?"*

"Corlan. What's it like there?"

A slight smile began. “It’s beautiful—ethereal. The whole world is alive with purple vegetation—flowers, vines, ferns, fungi, in hundreds of shades There’s only a few bodies of water—no seas, only shallow crystal lakes that appear lavender. Mist in the mornings, sometimes in the evenings, as well. Calm, tranquil. Inexplicable. Something more to be experienced than described.”

“I’ve always wanted to go there.”

“Perhaps you shall,” Cynara said, then yawned as exhaustion claimed her.

“You’re tired,” Travis said. “Go ahead and sleep. I’ll keep watch.” He slid back, easing himself almost flat against the boulder.

She nodded, stretched out near the fire, and pulled her cloak tighter. Linhok approached and settled protectively between Cynara and Travis. Her injured hand throbbed, but she thrust the pain aside until deep, dreamless sleep took hold.

Chapter Thirteen

FACING THE AFTERMATH

"Bumbling fool!"

Damon Maltron cringed inwardly but maintained his professional demeanor as Haburn shrieked. Ever since the Heliotians arrived, the governor had been on edge.

Haburn crashed his fist down on the marble-topped desk. "Is it so difficult, Maltron, to capture one frail girl?" He frowned, his mouth twisting into a distasteful leer as he appraised Maltron's battle-scarred appearance.

Shoulders back and rigid, Maltron faced his boss in a classic military stance. His face and hair were streaked with dirt, his clothing ripped and stained, blood caked on his cheek where the girl's vinte had sliced.

Coming directly to the governor to report failure, Maltron hadn't stopped to clean up. He held his emotions in check and kept his response neutral. "If she were alone, it would not have been a problem, sir, but an animal was with her. White as the clouds it was, sir. Some type of wild cat, only fiercer than any I've seen before. Even Y'rak was no match for it, especially when the others joined the fight."

"Others?" Haburn picked up immediately. "Explain. Where is Y'rak?"

"There were two others, sir—not with them but arriving just when our attack team believed we had things well in hand. At first, I thought the white beast was with them, but they seemed afraid of it also. They were a strange pair—a young fellow and a huge colored bird, the likes of which I've never seen before. The bird attacked first, giving the beast the advantage against Y'rak. The boy wasn't strong, but he hindered us enough that I couldn't reach the princess before she found shelter. By the time I had another chance, the beast had killed Y'rak and was coming after me—"

"Y'rak's dead?" Haburn interrupted, alarm in his voice.

"I'm afraid so, sir."

Haburn's face turned sickly white, and he sank into his chair as if his knees had turned to jelly. "Oh, help us, Tiel. Y'rak's dead… The alien witch will be furious… What of the others? Could they not help?"

Maltron gazed toward the floor. "They're all dead, sir."

"Dead? You're the only survivor?" His voice rose, disbelief evident. "Y'rak and the others dead…" He rubbed his face and leaned his elbows on the desk, muttering. "Eight men—six of them aliens—and only you returned."

Haburn seemed to drift off in thought as Maltron rolled his shoulders to ease the tension, wishing for this to be over. He couldn't change what had happened, and the failure was his to bear. Everyone had underestimated the princess's power and didn't factor in the damn cat.

Abruptly, Haburn's head shot up. "The skimmers… What of the skimmers?"

"Left behind, damaged. I had to coax mine back."

"By the Light of Corlan," Haburn swore loudly. "Y'riel will require retribution for this. You should hope, Maltron, that she will accept material payment and does not expect your life."

Maltron swallowed hard, his Adam's apple bobbing. "Surely, she wouldn't—?"

"She will demand whatever she pleases. However, I shall do my best to persuade her of your value to the plan's success. We still need to acquire the princess." He waved his hand in dismissal.

Maltron saluted stiffly and retreated, leaving the governor staring at a paper with trembling hands.

He doubted Haburn could dissuade the empress from ordering his death. He had already witnessed her cold anger, once directed at him. Haburn was playing a dangerous game, betting against the princess and the Clan of Cantra. Maltron didn't like the odds.

AT HOME, DAMON MALTRON poured a large goblet of sunberry wine, his second, and relaxed on the davenport. He'd showered and applied healing ointment to his cuts and bruises. Physically, he felt better. Mentally, he suffered torture. Knowing how the Heliotians responded to failure, he did not anticipate a pleasant experience ahead.

Failure… failure…

Why was it so difficult to capture one teenage girl? Sorceress or not, she was still just a kid. But she had unleashed a burst of light and wind—power beyond anything he expected.

With a sharp jerk of his head, he poked a button built into the arm of the davenport and spoke quietly. *"Selection eighteen, control eight."* He needed distraction.

Immediately, his household computer searched the music tapes in control box eight until it found the desired selection. The sound of the Minoan zitheria—atonal, multi-octave—filled the room, and Damon closed his eyes.

His apartment was exceptional: a large flat on the fifth floor of Suedjal Towers. Floor-to-ceiling drapes opened to an impressive view of the Tark Lonan boat landing. Haburn paid him well, but now Maltron reconsidered the arrangement.

He sold his services—for a high price. Until now, working for Haburn had been rewarding, but this last assignment had been dirtier than usual. He disliked Haburn's alliance with the aliens altogether.

It's not right to side with them against the Aramans and possibly the whole Astara system. Especially when the price of failure is so high. Not that he feared death, but he didn't care for executions.

With a deep, regretful sigh, he gulped another swig of wine and gazed solemnly around his apartment. He'd called this home for seven years, nearly a quarter of his life. He enjoyed the luxury—the sound system, the automatic dining center, the magnificent river view. He would miss it, but he saw no alternative except to leave. Haburn would not stand up to the Heliotian empress; Maltron knew that for certain. His future was nonexistent.

Where to go? An amused expression crossed his suntanned face as he recalled the beautiful Corlanish Princess. She needed protection if the trio who rescued her were all she had. He touched his cheek ruefully, acknowledging she fought roughly, but he didn't hold it against her. She may only be a girl, but she was a tigress. Being her bodyguard might be a pleasant task—but how to approach her?

He still mulled over the idea when the comm-console began beeping. He noted the caller's displayed name. Clarinda. Another regret. Their relationship required change; she was becoming too possessive. He ignored the call, silencing the machine.

His finger hovered over it a moment, then summoned the household computer again. "Selection thirty-two, control fifty-eight."

There was a long delay as the computer searched, then a thin metallic voice issued from the speaker. "Selection thirty-two, control fifty-eight is not available at the moment. You are number fifteen."

Figures. It was a new selection, already popular. He wouldn't wait that long. "Cancel request."

He finished his wine in one large gulp, then padded to his closet to select suitable clothing.

What did one wear to an interview with a sorceress?

Chapter Fourteen

Time For a Change

THE PITCH-BLACK ALLEYWAY stretched for an entire block, a corridor of unyielding metal between two towering buildings. Not even the light from the double moons reached to illuminate it. Damon Maltron pressed a guiding hand against one wall and followed it quickly and silently to the recessed door on his right. Pulling an electronically encoded card from his pocket, he inserted it into the slot above the lock. He waited as a series of clicks cycled, repeated, and the door popped open while simultaneously ejecting his card. His movement displayed more confidence than he felt; his nervous fingers slipped the card back into his pocket. Taking a deep breath, he stepped inside.

Ahead stretched a softly illuminated hallway leading to a walkway above a small hangar. Maltron knew the route well, so he didn't pause. His sharp hearing detected the guard even before the man spoke.

"Halt and identify!"

Maltron turned toward the speaker, raising his hands. Although the guard's weapon was illegal on Arama, the man knew how to use it—but he wasn't trigger-happy.

"Maltron, Damon. Special aide to—"

"Maltron! What the blazes are you doing here at this hour?"

"Special assignment." Damon stepped forward as the guard switched on a flashlight. Just his luck—it was Klacquer, a guard he knew well. "How are you doing, Klacquer?"

"Oh, I'm getting by. I wasn't notified you'd be here." Klacquer sounded uncertain, uneasy at regulations not being followed.

Damon hastened to assure him. "Top secret. It's a special job for the governor, and he didn't want to broadcast it, if you get my meaning. Wants me to take an alien skimmer out." He glanced over the railing. "I see the scout ship hasn't returned."

Klacquer fell in step alongside him as he made his way toward the stairs. "Nah, it's still not in, but it shouldn't be too much longer. I get the creeps every time one comes in, and those creatures get out. I may get paid well to ignore them, but it still doesn't seem right."

"Yeah, I know what you mean." Damon unlocked the dome of the skimmer—the same one he'd used earlier. "You ever see the inside of one of these? Take a look. Odd controls, a little cramped, but more efficient than the Minoan vehicles."

Hesitantly, Klacquer leaned forward to peer at the alien contraption. "I tell you, I don't much trust anything those buggers bring here. But you've taken one for a drive, haven't you?"

"Yeah, I have. When you figure them out, they're a lot like ours."

Once the man leaned in far enough, Damon moved quickly. He slammed the dome down hard, catching Klacquer's neck between the edges of metal. A muffled cry, several jerks of the pinned body—and then silence.

Feeling queasy, Damon looked away and took several deep breaths. *He'd killed before, but it was never easy, especially when the victim was an acquaintance, and the means so crude.* Regrettable, but vital to his plan. Opening the dome again, he checked to be certain Klacquer was dead, then shoved the body into the vehicle. The task was awkward; Klacquer was nearly his size and heavier.

Panting, he leaned against the skimmer, checked his time, and relaxed. This step was complete. Now he needed to get away before the scout returned.

He maneuvered over the body and settled into the skimmer's small seat. He activated the automatic door, pressed the coded sequence, and guided it carefully into the tunnel the governor had ordered constructed for these vehicles. Keeping altitude low in case the scout was inbound, Damon opened the throttle as full as he dared and tried not to think of the consequences.

His fears proved unjustified. He zipped down the tunnel and out into the night with no problems. Immediately altering course to the east, he pointed the skimmer toward the Sun Mountains. He pulled out the tracker he'd linked to Y'rak's embedded signal and followed it. While the Princess and her companions might have moved from that position, he figured they would be near there. His tracking skills exceeded average. He'd find them.

Damon Maltron reached the foothills, where he'd been just hours earlier, shortly before sunrise. He didn't take the skimmer all the way; it was too risky. He landed about a mile from where he estimated the princess would camp, removed a few items he'd brought with him, and scowled at the body of the guard. Moving the corpse was awkward but necessary, and it took more effort than he cared to spend to shift it behind the controls of the skimmer. He took the identification card from Klacquer's pocket and replaced it with his own.

The next part was trickier. Maltron started the vehicle, set the controls, and pointed it at a tree a hundred yards ahead. With a deep breath, he released the brake, leaped back, and tumbled onto the grass, rolling away.

The skimmer bolted forward, lurched wildly, then crashed into the tree at an angle. Flames burst from the engine, engulfing it in a red-gold fountain that quickly consumed any flammable materials.

Grimly, Maltron hoisted his bundle and turned away. With luck, when the Heliotians found the wreck and the guard's body, they would assume Maltron had crashed. By the time they discovered the truth, he'd be safely away.

Before heading deeper into the foothills, Maltron detoured to the site of the skirmish. The ground was scarred—burnt brush, gouged earth—but no bodies lay in sight. He crouched, running his fingers over the disturbed soil. Someone had buried them. The princess, perhaps, or her companions. Even the alien corpses had been given rest.

For a long moment he stood in silence, uneasy. He had fought beside Y'rak, despised him, yet still felt the weight of seeing his grave. With a grunt, he gathered the few remains scattered nearby and covered them with earth. It was crude, but it was something.

Straightening, he scanned the horizon. Tracks led away from the site—skimmer ruts, broken brush, faint signs of passage. He followed them, step by step, until the hazy curl of smoke against the dawn sky gave him direction. The trail pointed him toward the camp.

As he hiked, he pondered what he'd say to the princess. Haburn thought little of her magical skill, but she'd impressed him. His eyes still felt gritty from the dirt she'd conjured and hurled at him. She'd defended herself well, far more than he'd expected. Her control might be weak, but it had been enough to avoid capture. If she'd been alone, he might have overcome her—but not easily. So how to convince her he wanted to join her side? He could tell her the truth, but would it be enough?

The terrain was low hills, easy going. Maltron made good time, though the camp was farther than he'd estimated. He was questioning his instincts when he spotted the small encampment. If not for the breaking dawn, he might have missed it.

Gambling on a non-violent reception, Maltron walked directly toward the camp. About thirty yards away from the youth's reclining figure, he heard the growl behind him. He froze, memory vivid of the giant cat's ability. The hairs on his neck rose. He forced himself to remain calm, lifted his arms to show empty hands. *Maybe he'd miscalculated.*

TRAVIS HEARD A LOW GROWL near his ears and rolled toward the sound. He barely glimpsed the silently disappearing frost leopard, but he came to full alert. A snap of a branch caught his attention, bringing his eyes to the dark form moving in the brush near their camp.

When Linhok moved into position behind the stranger, Travis rose and went forward to meet the intruder. He knew Linhok would attack if the stranger made any attempt to hurt him or the princess. He stopped about five feet away and ran his eyes over the man, who also halted and waited. Their visitor stood at least three inches taller than Travis, was much broader-shouldered, and undoubtedly stronger. He was doubtless armed; Travis concluded and issued a warning. "Don't come any closer unless you want a very large cat on your shoulder."

The man remained in position, not moving. Travis watched him, waiting to see if he would speak. When he didn't, he said, "Who are you, and what are you doing here?"

"I wish to speak to Princess Cynara. I have a proposition for her."

"What makes you think the princess is here?"

"Let's just say I have my ways of knowing, and that's all you need to know. Anything else I have to say, I'll say to the lady herself, so please tell her I'm here."

Travis studied the man, admiring the way he stood defiantly against the cat's watchful eyes. He either had a great deal of courage or was an idiot. Still, he hesitated to take him to Cynara. "Put any weapons, including knives, on the ground. Raise your hands above your head and keep them there. If you lay a hand on me, Linhok will go for your throat."

As the man complied and set a laser weapon and two long-bladed knives down before him, Travis walked forward and halted right in front. Oddly, he didn't feel the threat had been a total bluff; he was confident Linhok would do something if the stranger moved to harm him. He bent to pick up the laser gun, noting it was fully charged. The weapon was illegal and the first one he had ever seen. Without a word, Travis stuck the gun under his own belt, picked up the knives, and stepped back, facing the intruder.

Now what? Take him to Cynara? Travis doubted the wisdom of that move. A few heartbeats later, he was relieved of the decision.

AWAKENED WHEN LINHOK DETECTED the stranger, Cynara remained quiet while her leopard investigated. Pleased that Travis showed the courage to confront the man, she waited until he'd disarmed their visitor before she stepped out from the edge of the clearing and walked toward them, stopping by Travis' side. "I am Princess Cynara. You are?"

"Damon Maltron, at your service, my Lady."

She detected more than of hint of cockiness in his voice. He was not a man to humble himself with anyone. "Indeed. And what do you plan to do in my service?"

"I could serve as your bodyguard, and I have other … talents to offer."

"Indeed?" Cynara repeated, an eyebrow lifting to an arch. "You may lower your hands now but keep them visible." She waited as Maltron dropped his hands and let them rest by his hips. "Might I inquire what these 'talents' are?"

Maltron shifted his weight. "I'm skilled with fighting devices and techniques. I can move quickly and quietly, and I'm an excellent observer."

"What makes you think I need a bodyguard?"

"I think that's obvious, my Lady. A woman such as yourself is likely to be the target of many, and you seem to be short of adequate protection." He cast a glance at Travis and tilted his head in Linhok's direction.

"I can protect her," Travis said, his voice gruff. Cynara saw the anger in his eyes as his jaw visibly tightened.

Maltron looked amused but said nothing.

"How did you find me, Siri Maltron?"

"I have contacts in the right places—another bonus with my services."

"I'll bet you do." Cynara recognized him, even though his face had been covered before. She couldn't mistake that build and the arrogant-sounding voice. He'd made a painful impression on her. So why was he here? Aloud, she asked, "And what would your services cost?"

"Very little—compared to your life. I wish to be provided with an excellent apartment in the city and a reasonable amount to live on—say two hundred fifty *tracas* a week."

Travis's mouth dropped open in astonishment. "Two hundred fifty tracas? That's a small fortune!"

"Oh, but I am well worth it." Maltron countered immediately. "Besides, that's up to her ladyship to accept or decline."

Cynara's mouth spread to a tight smile. "You have a great deal of confidence in yourself. It's strange, but I feel as if I've met you before. Is that possible?"

"I don't believe so."

Lie. This man had attacked her earlier, intending to either kill or abduct her. Was he changing sides or trying to get closer to succeed in his assignment? "Tell me, where are you from, and where did you provide services before coming to me?"

"Tark Lonan," he replied without pause. "I was working for the regional government until last night. I decided I needed to change employers."

That much was true, but it wasn't the complete story. Cynara gazed at him for several heartbeats, deciding if she should accept his services or reject him outright.

If she took him on, he would be closer but would need to be watched. If she pushed him away, he would come after her as an enemy, for sure.

So, what do you think, Linhok? Bring the potential assassin into our fold where we can see him or leave him free to strike from afar?

I do not like either option, Lady. If I must choose, bring him close where I can observe him.

Agreed. Cynara thrust her shoulders back and looked Maltron in the eyes. "Very well, Siri Maltron. I will employ you, although I should warn you now that we face grave dangers and may not survive at all. Or, if I do, I may not be in a position to pay your salary.

"Furthermore, you will be a member of my escort group. As for personal bodyguards, I already have two, and they are quite capable. I noticed you did not test their ability."

Maltron tilted his head slightly. "Well put, Lady. I will accept your terms of employment, and I assure you I will do everything in my power to protect your entire party."

Travis started to retort, but Cynara's hand fell gently yet firmly on his arm, and he swallowed his words, accepting her decision as final. She turned back toward the camp, walking confidently as if she had not hired an unknown liability into her service. She could see Travis felt nervous about it as he fell into step with her, and Maltron followed him.

When she glanced backward, she confirmed she had no worries about the mercenary in their midst; Linhok guarded the rear, and the cat's eyes never left the newcomer's back.

Chapter Fifteen

Betrayal at Tark Lonan

GOVERNOR HABURN APPEARED CALM as he waited at his desk for the search party he'd sent after Maltron to report in. Across from him, the alien Empress sat ramrod-straight in a high-backed chair. She was displeased with the loss of three of her vehicles, her warriors—especially Y'rak— and the disappearance of the man who had failed, once again, to apprehend the princess.

A knock at the door announced the arrival of the lead searcher. He marched in, paid brief respect to the Empress, then saluted Haburn.

"We found a wrecked skimmer, sir. It hit a tree and caught fire. We couldn't identify the charred body, but we found Maltron's identity card and presume it was him. We recorded all the details."

"Very well," Haburn said, accepting the metal card to be adequate proof. "You are dismissed."

His gaze shifted to the Empress. Her mouth had tightened into a grim line. The destroyed one was the third of the Heliotian skimmers.

"I regret the loss of your vehicles, Majesty." He still wasn't sure how she wished to be addressed, but majesty seemed safe.

"At least the incompetent man will not bother us anymore. I only regret losing the transport. Enough of that—we have more business to attend. Are you ready, Governor?"

He swallowed hard, not liking what he needed to do next. He wasn't sure how his constituents would receive the announcement. "Yes. I will meet you at the South Veranda."

Empress Y'riel rose, gave him a nod, and strode from his office with her guards surrounding her.

A SHORT TIME LATER, Y'riel stood beside Haburn to officially take her first city. *No battle, no losses, an easy surrender.* Haburn would publicly yield the metropolis he'd promised to her. Still, she was accompanied by her small, select group of warriors, who constantly shifted to protect her. As she strode down the hall, her elaborate red and gold ceremonial robe swirled with each step, revealing the lightweight but effective armor covering her body.

This was a momentous occasion for her and for her *hiverot* nestors. The city itself was minor, but the symbolism immense. It was handed over, a model for how many of her victories would be achieved after Ama City fell. She had already decided to accelerate the conquest once the organisms in the water spread faster than expected. She was anxious to proceed.

Haburn stepped to the podium and gazed at the restless crowd gathered in the square below the outdoor veranda. Audio-visual pickups would broadcast the ceremony to the small group of administrators assembled in the Town Hall. He thrust his shoulders back and, in an authoritative voice, addressed them.

"My friends and supporters, one of the responsibilities of the governorship of the city is to provide protection and safety for its citizens. A few divisions ago, I learned of a planned invasion of our world by an alien race, a people not unlike us. My main concerns were the safety of my city, my friends, and all of you. With this in mind, I made the necessary contacts to communicate with these aliens.

"It is my belief Corlan cannot protect us against this invasion, and in fact, Princess Cynara, the official representative of the Clan of Cantra on Arama, has not even responded to my requests to speak with her about a matter I considered of the utmost importance. I have seen the alien world, and I have seen their weapons. I have been there. You can believe me when I tell you it is my opinion that we cannot fight these people. With the poisoning of the water surrounding Ama City, we are seeing only the first of their attack. We will soon see the full impact of their power."

Murmurs rippled through the crowd. Nervous looks passed from one to another. Haburn raised his hands, palms out, and lowered them a couple of times. "Peace, my friends. Let me continue." The murmuring settled, and many eyes turned to Y'riel, who stood rigid in her finery, a dozen paces from the governor.

"I should say Ama City will see their powerful force, as will any other cities choosing to resist the conquest. Tark Lonan will not be a resistant city. Tark Lonan will not be a destroyed city. I have taken the lead in this. Tark Lonan will be spared because I have reached an agreement with the Exalted Empress Y'riel. This compact will ensure the safety of this city and its citizens."

Haburn took a deep breath, raised the city staff beside him, and declared: "I now surrender the city of Tark Lonan to the Empress Y'riel of Helios in exchange for the safety of the city and all our people."

Fierce-looking in her ceremonial robes, Y'riel marched to stand beside Haburn. Muffled clicks accompanied her when the plates of her armor touched edges under her robes. Spreading her arms wide, she brought her head up, and the dark irises of her eyes nearly filled the entire sockets.

With a powerful voice, she addressed the people of Tark Lonan in hesitant Araman. "I take this city for my first conquest on this world and claim it for the Empire of Helios. I accept this city under the terms set forth by Governor Haburn. It will be a peaceful takeover so long as no one resists. Even now, my warriors are in the streets of the city, but they will harm no one unless there is trouble."

Inside the Hall, muffled comments rose but no outburst. Shocked, the people were thinking about what they'd just witnessed. Haburn had judged them well: they believed cooperation offered more than resistance.

Outside, the crowd reacted violently. Repelled by the Empress's alien appearance, they shouted objections and disgust. Many grabbed whatever they could as weapons.

From doorways and alleys stepped heavily armed Helios troops. A large, muscled man charged with a splint of wood. He never reached his target. A warrior fired a beam that dropped him instantly. Behind him, another man leapt to attack, likewise felled. Others hesitated, dropped their makeshift weapons, and backed away. An alien stepped forward, voice gruff and unnatural, ordering them to disperse.

Reluctantly, the people obeyed. As they returned to shops and homes, they muttered: *Where was the Clan of Cantra? Why hadn't they done something? Why hadn't the Princess come to help us?*

Y'riel's lips curved slightly at the declaration. She had no concerns about the Clan. They had done nothing to prevent her arrival. Still, she would make them the next target after Ama City. Yes, her decision to accelerate the invasion was a good one.

She turned to the officer standing next to her. "Advise Y'van to commence his attack on the capital city." He saluted and left to follow her order.

She turned to Haburn. "You have done well, Governor. You will hold your position here, reporting to me. I go now to join my troops, but I leave Y'Nost as my representative. My warriors will remain to thwart any other resistance."

"Yes, your Majesty," Haburn replied, bobbing his head in deference.

Y'riel turned away and marched back inside to prepare for the trip to Ama City. *With luck, Y'van will have secured the city before I arrive.*

Reluctantly, the people obeyed. As they returned to shops and homes, they muttered. Where was the Dragon Castle? Why hadn't they done something? Why hadn't the Princess come to help us?

[illegible] She had no concerns about the Clan. They had done nothing to prevent her arrival. Still, she would make them the next target after [illegible] City. Yes, her [illegible] the invasion was a good one.

She turned to the officer standing next to her. "Advise [illegible] to commence his attack on the capital city." He saluted and left to follow her order.

She turned to Habirn. "You have done well, Governor. [illegible] will hold your position here. [illegible] to me. I go now to [illegible] my troops, but [illegible] as my representative. [illegible] will remain to [illegible] any [illegible] resistance."

"Yes, your Majesty," Habirn replied, bowing his head in deference.

She [illegible] away and marched back to [illegible] to prepare for the trip to [illegible] City. With luck, [illegible] would have secured [illegible] before [illegible]

Chapter Sixteen

Regroup and Repair

CAN EITHER OF THEM be repaired?" Cynara asked, leaning over Travis's shoulder as he tinkered with the alien skimmer. He'd already surveyed her damaged vehicle and reckoned it could be repaired if he could cannibalize enough compatible parts off the other alien ones. Although the designs were similar, the skimmers were entirely different –controls, power units, body materials, everything.

Travis sat back, slapped his hand against the energy pod, and frowned. "I might be able to repair this one if I can figure out the connector sequence to the energy pods. They don't look like the Minoan-manufactured ones, and I'm not even sure what the energy source is. Still, if the pods connections are similar, I should be able to match them up."

As he worked the cover off the alien skimmer's energy pod, a peculiar acrid odor like burnt grain almost choked him. Coughing a few times, he drew a breath and he touched the pod gingerly. His fingers pulled back and lightly returned, shoulders shaking. "This thing has a weird energy vibration," he said through gritted teeth.

Cynara nodded. "Yes, it does. The alien power surges through it. I don't want to touch it again." She recalled the feeling too clearly. She looked away, her attention shifting to Maltron standing several feet away from them, keeping watch while they attempted to get the two skimmers working again. The others were in worse shape, so their hopes rested with scavenged parts and Travis's skill.

How much could they trust Maltron?

Cynara left Travis to work, settled herself in the shade of a *riji* tree, closed her eyes, and attempted to rest. Beneath her calm exterior, she tried to set aside the insistent pain from her battered hand and send her astral force to Ama City. She felt an urgent need to know the situation in her capital city, but the agony of the injury would not be willed away, and she couldn't pull free of her body. Her shoulders slumped as her head dropped forward, weary with the effort.

Are you all right, my Lady? Linhok inquired.

Yes, Linhok. I just can't pull free of this physical pain. I almost wish you'd remained in Ama City so I could at least get a report through you.

I would not have much knowledge--just what I could discover from your chambers, Linhok replied sensibly.

No, you could have gotten out of your special passage and into the city proper. But there's no point in speculating on it now. I've been tricked, Linhok, and I fell for it.

There was no need to go to Tark Lonan?

No. No need at all. It has already fallen to the enemy.

You've seen? Been there?

No, I know, that's all. There was betrayal in Tark Lonan. She glanced toward Maltron. *That one, Linhok,—Maltron. Do you sense anything from him?*

Affirmative, but I cannot isolate it.

Nor I. Watch him closely, she ordered.

Linhok's ears flicked as a spasm of pain cut through Cynara's thoughts. She bit her lip even as she caught her breath.

Nearby, Travis brought his head up as he heard her gasp. His hand barely missed connecting with the edge of the energy pod, which could have proven dangerous. "Are you all right, Cynara?"

She nodded; face scrunched in pain. "It's just my hand."

Swinging his head toward Maltron, Travis said, "Say, man of many talents, can you manage a fire?"

"I believe so," Maltron replied. He glanced to where the princess watched him, and he smiled slightly, then set about the task.

Travis shook his head, crossed to stand closer to the princess, and wiped his hands on his pants. "When Zeldana returns with the berries, I'll mix a drink to ease the pain. Why don't you try to rest some more?" He reached for her cloak, knelt, and draped it around her shoulders.

When his arm rested lightly on her back, Cynara dropped her head against it, wanting the contact. Automatically, he pulled her closer into his arms, and she shifted until her head rested against his chest.

Just for a bit, she thought. She needed to feel the bit of comfort he offered.

Her lips pulled into a tight line instead of their earlier fullness. Her own healing ability failed to help with the broken hand.

"Your hand might be infected," Travis said. "The berries will help with the pain, but they won't heal the wound."

Cynara gained some strength from the youth's touch, or perhaps it was just knowing he was near and she was not alone in this. Forcing herself to move from the comfort of his arms, she touched his cheek briefly with the fingertips of her good hand and forced a smile. "Thank you, Travis, but please, return to the skimmers. It's vital I get back to Ama City."

As he returned to the task, an amused smirk pulled her lips. Funny, she'd thought of him as a boy when they met, yet he was older than she. Their lives were different, but he was no less a young man for it.

Leaning back, she closed her eyes and tried to take her mind off what might be happening in Ama City.

TRAVIS NODDED AND RELUCTANTLY returned to his attempts to repair the skimmer, but doubts gnawed at him. None of the combinations he'd tried had worked. He suspected the alien power source would not be usable with the Minoan vehicle, but he had to keep trying. Whoever built this skimmer had a totally different concept than the Minoan engineers.

Abruptly, the torn face of the alien flashed in his mind, and he shuddered at the touch of the vehicle.

Frustrated, he threw the knife he'd been using as a tool to the ground. It was no use. He couldn't do anything with only a knife. He needed tools to work with and scanners to get technical readouts. He might make this work with those, but not this way.

His gaze drifted toward the north, where Marglen lay little more than a mile away. Even though it was just a small farm community, it would have tools and maybe a healer. "I could go to Marglen for tools, but they're likely to be expensive," he told the Princess.

"Would the town have what you need to fix the machines?"

"Possibly. And it might have a healer, too."

"No, not here," she said firmly. "I can't let anyone in this area know I'm here. Can you send Maltron for what you need?"

“I guess. I'll make a list.” He didn't like the idea of sending Maltron, but he also didn't want to leave the princess alone. “I don't have enough credits to buy—”

Cynara forced a wan smile. “A compartment in my skimmer, next to the seat, has a credit voucher for the palace. It doesn't require a signature to use. It should have enough on it for anything you need.”

With reluctance, he approached Maltron and explained his mission, giving him a list of specific tools to buy and the voucher. Even though the mercenary grunted his agreement, he seemed none too pleased with going into town. Nonetheless, he set off at a quick pace.

Hearing the flutter of wings, Travis turned from Maltron's departing back to greet Zeldana. The kyereagle bore a berry-covered branch in her beak and waited anxiously for Travis to take it from her. He recognized them at once. "Exactly what I wanted, Zeldana. You're marvelous."

"Do you have any idea how much searching it took to find those? It's a good thing my eyesight is superior, friend Travis, or I would still be searching." The kyereagle puffed up importantly.

"Yes, I know they're hard to find," Travis agreed, "but these are very special. The princess will feel much better after I make a drink from these little berries." He hurried off to put the dark red fruit in a pan. With a glance toward Zeldana as she waddled to follow, he asked, "Did you spot anything else?"

"Just the usual activity. Except—" Zeldana hesitated.

Travis paused in crushing the berries to encourage her. "Except what?"

"Maybe it was my imagination, but I thought I saw a glimpse of silver in the sky. It was a large object—oblong in shape, but it was only visible a moment before it disappeared from view in the sun's reflection."

Almost dropping the pan of crushed berries, Travis turned to the bird. "A silver object? Was it a ship, Zeldana?"

The bird preened at her wing. "A ship? You mean an inter-planets ship? No, I don't think so. It wasn't that large--more like a shuttle, but not like any I've seen before. Besides, I only got a glimpse."

Cynara approached, her eyes alert and focused on the bird. "You lost view of it in the sun's reflection, Zeldana? Which direction was it going?"

Zeldana cocked her head. "I believe it was to the west, but I couldn't say for sure."

Cynara gazed toward the sky, thinking about the possibilities. "Zeldana, are you familiar with which shuttle types fly into Arama?"

"I've seen several of them, Princess. This object did not look like one."

Cynara nodded, then.

It's probably like the one I saw. Not Minoan." Travis said.

Cynara's voice was not quite a whisper when she breathed out. "A squid-like body with trailing fins resembling tentacles. The aliens are near." She returned to her spot under the tree.

TRAVIS RESUMED HIS BERRY PREPARATION, heating the crushed pulp and juices in a pan, adding some herbs his mother had sent with him. He poured the liquid into a mug and handed it to Cynara. "This should numb the pain. The berries have a pain killer in them."

She accepted the mug and sipped. "Ah, sweet, not bitter. I didn't expect that. It has an unusual taste, but not unpleasant. You're a wonder, Travis. A mechanic, a cook, and a healer—a man of many skills."

He beamed at the praise, feeling for the first time as if he'd come into his own, an independent man and a guard to the sorceress herself. Modestly, he said, "I really don't know all that much, Cynara, but my mother did teach me about healing herbs and berries. As for mechanics, any farmer can do it, but I do have a natural gift for design."

"Design?"

At the show of interest, Travis launched into telling her about his plans to go to the University. Before long, he was babbling with enthusiasm, and she listened until she nodded off to sleep. As he resumed his repair tasks, he wondered when, or if, he would make it to Weilock Center.

Chapter Seventeen

TRUTH OR PREMONITION

OVER TWO HOURS LATER, twilight deepened as Damon Maltron slipped back into camp, almost unnoticed except for a piercing glance from the frost leopard. He misread the pained look on Cynara's face, thinking her hand was bothering her, and felt a twinge of guilt.

Why should this get to me? She tried to kill me too. Yesterday she was a target; today I work for her. Strange fate—but the only sensible move. Staying in Tark Lonan would have been suicide, and the Princess was the one most likely to employ someone like me.

She and Travis sat by the fire. She leaned against a cushion of cloaks stuffed between her and a log. Damon studied her face—beautiful, youthful in some ways, far older in others. It unsettled him that he'd hurt her. He wasn't accustomed to feeling guilt.

He stepped into the clearing as Linhok snarled to announce his presence. Travis glanced up, then returned his attention to the princess. Cynara's features looked more relaxed, the pain subdued.

"Those berries are finally working. I was beginning to worry they wouldn't." Travis raised his eyes to Damon. "Her hand has multiple breaks, and one's torn through the skin." He lifted her hand, unwrapped the bandage, and cleaned the wound.

Damon saw the swelling, the discoloration, blood seeping where bone broke through. Other scrapes marred her skin. *Too bad she hadn't used her telekinetic skills to clear the path.*

Travis applied a fresh bandage, smiling faintly when she appeared to sleep. Rising, he faced Maltron, who handed him a heavy package.

"I couldn't get everything," Maltron said. "They didn't have much stock, but it might be enough to repair the skimmers."

Travis sorted through the parts. "I wish they'd had a scanlite," he muttered.

Cynara mumbled through the berry haze, "Do the best you can. It's imperative we get to Ama City before the aliens."

"Aliens?" Maltron feigned surprise. "Do you think there are aliens in Ama City?" He laughed, forcing the sound.

Cynara's tired gaze slid to him. "Yes, Siri Maltron. Our enemy comes from another star."

Maltron didn't laugh again. "You're positive, your Highness?"

"Yes. We buried one yesterday."

She turned to Travis. "Get back to the machines. It's vital we move."

Travis sighed. "This will take a miracle, and Maltron didn't bring one back."

Maltron shifted uneasily. Waiting made him nervous. Repairs could take hours, and even then, one skimmer wouldn't carry them all. He stood, gazed toward the pass, and said, "I'll scout ahead while we're delayed here. I won't be gone long." Without confirmation, he slipped into the woods, avoiding the road.

THROUGH SLITTED EYES, CYNARA watched him go, groggy thoughts circling. *Why did he join us?*

"Zeldana could do a better job of scouting," Travis muttered, pulling a panel off the skimmer.

"Yes, but Maltron needs action. He's restless."

"I don't trust him." He squinted into the wiring. "This is going to be tough in the dark."

With a wry grin, Cynara conjured a ball of light, directing it to his work. "This should help. I have doubts too, but safer to keep him with us than with someone who opposes me. Don't worry; we'll watch him closely." She closed her eyes again. Linhok had already shadowed him.

Now that the ache in her hand had dulled, she thought she might block it out enough to astral travel. Leaning back, she breathed deeply, relaxed each part of her body, and concentrated. Incense and crystals helped, but she could do without them if she focused.

In her mind, she built Ama City—its sky-pillar towers, squat buildings, bustling streets, peddlers with carts, children and animals. She added life until the vision became reality.

Her first glimpse seemed normal, but then she spotted a hooded figure moving like he belonged to the shadows. With a mere desire, she shifted to see his face: high-cheeked, yellow-skinned, dark slanted eyes squinting toward the palace. *My palace.*

She moved swiftly through corridors to her sealed door. The guard was on duty, the force field intact. Relief. Inside her chambers, she saw the blue flashing of the telescreen from Corlan. She couldn't answer in this form, but it was not a good sign.

Through the wall into the inner courtyard, she saw what she feared. In the eastern sky, six huge airships approached faster than anything she'd ever seen. Within moments, they descended over the city, under sides barely clearing the tallest towers. Fire streaked down into streets and buildings.

People screamed and fled; animals bolted into alleys. The air crackled as defense shields snapped on, delayed by faulty sensors. She knew they wouldn't hold long. The ships turned for another pass.

MALTRON RETURNED FROM HIS scouting expedition and stopped short when he saw Cynara. She sat unnaturally still, head drooping against the log, her body slack as if lifeless. He stepped closer, uneasy.

"What's she doing?"

"Don't touch her," Travis warned. "She's in a trance." He rose from the skimmer, tossed a bolt-spinner aside, and muttered, "I can't make progress with these. Not without more parts."

"Trance?" Maltron echoed, ignoring the complaint. "She really does that? Are you sure it isn't just a reaction to that juice you gave her?"

Travis shook his head, a smug look flashing. "No. She's using her power. That's why they call her a sorceress."

Maltron shifted uneasily. "Sure, I've heard the stories… Who hasn't? But I never believed it. You've seen her do this before?"

"Last night."

"She does it whenever she wants?"

Travis's gaze returned to the Princess, concern etched in the lines of his forehead. "I don't think it's easy for her, and it leaves her vulnerable."

"What does she do in these trances?"

Travis shrugged. "I'm not sure, but she gains knowledge somehow."

Maltron frowned. "She looks drugged to me."

A sound behind them snapped both men around. Maltron dropped into a defensive crouch, a hand reaching for his weapon. Linhok stood five yards away, an alphare hanging limply from his jaws.

Travis relaxed and strode forward. "My Lady's dinner," he murmured, taking the animal from the leopard's jaws.

Unconcerned with the men, Linhok padded to lie beside his mistress and wait. Moments later, unintelligible muttering from Cynara warned she was returning to herself. Linhok licked her hand.

Rolling to one side, she tucked into a tight circle, arms pulled in for protection. Fatigue showed on her face, her eyes barely open. She looked … drained.

Travis set the dead animal down on a rock before turning back to the skimmer he'd been working on. "Dinner can wait. I almost have this one working."

MID-MORNING FOUND THEM on the road, not as far along as Cynara had hoped to be.

From the top of the hills, Damon Maltron gazed at the road cutting through the valley below. Nothing moved along it. Traffic was never heavy on Arama's highways—most travelers preferred sky hoppers, far faster than ground vehicles. Most traffic came from giant transporters hauling goods, fuel, and food across the continent. Less often, personal vehicles used them to smooth the ride for pampered passengers. Only the elite had access to skimmers, those marvelous crafts able to take any path.

Damon reflected on the past twenty hours. He'd always been a fighter, sometimes a hired killer, his loyalties easily bought. But he'd never acted out of anger or hate—until now.

Turning, his gaze traveled to the plateau below. Cynara sat on a boulder, Travis knelt beside a small fire warming berry juice, the leopard lazed under a tree, tail flicking, and the bird had gone off to scout. Uneasily, Damon looked back to the road. He wasn't sure how he felt about the girl. She wasn't what he'd expected, and he couldn't stop thinking about her. *Business arrangement,* he reminded himself. *Nothing more.*

They had left camp at first light. Travis had coaxed two skimmers into working, but Cynara's sputtered out after two hours, and the alien vehicle faltered too. While Travis tinkered, Damon scouted ahead. Cynara had decided they would lose too much time with repairs. Better to try the highway, where they might catch a transport. Slower than skimmers, but steady.

They followed the highway at a distance, careful not to be seen. With her white-blonde hair and the white leopard, Cynara was an obvious target.

Damon's thoughts drifted back toward Tark Lonan. He doubted he had escaped cleanly. A trap was surely being laid. If he had remained in Haburn's employ, he would already be dead. The governor was a coward, and the aliens would win. Damon had seen their weapons. What did the Clan have? A princess with hand-to-hand skills, a leopard, and a boy dreaming of glory. *What chance do they have against Helios war machines?*

And he couldn't even tell Cynara what he knew without incriminating himself. Either way, he was a dead man unless he found a way off-planet. But even other worlds might fall. If the Clan had found ways to sustain life on desolate planets, so could the Heliotians. None of Astara's worlds were safe.

Still, if he had to die, he'd rather die fighting than be executed by the Empress. Despite his mercenary status, he felt an attachment to the land where he was born—and an inexplicable pull toward the Princess who had hired him. He pictured her again, lashes twitching as she reclined in trance. Vulnerable, perhaps, but not powerless. She was young, beautiful, but she ruled Arama. There had to be more to her. Otherwise, the tales of Corlan's sorcerers were fabrications. He chuckled. *Wouldn't that beat all if they'd fooled everyone with stories of power that never existed?*

The rumble of engines echoed through the valley. Damon recognized the sound instantly. Grain transports ran this valley route at dawn and dusk, carrying harvests from the mountain farms to the lowland depots. If luck held, this was the driver's usual run.

Hurrying back down the hill, he called out as soon as he was close enough. "Lady, there's a grain transport coming. It's on its regular route—farm to depot. We can stop it and borrow it to reach Ama City."

"Borrow it?" Cynara arched an eyebrow.

Maltron knelt to face her eye to eye. "Yes. Borrow it."

"What if the driver does not wish to loan it?"

"Then we take it. But I'm sure the driver will be pleased to loan it to Corlan's Princess."

Cynara sighed. "I don't believe we have any other choice. Go ahead and take it. Travis, assist him."

"I don't need help, your Highness. This is one of those special services of mine." He gave her a quick smile and a wink, then strode back up the hill.

CYNARA'S EYES FOLLOWED HIM for a few minutes as he picked an easy, fast path. "He's a stubborn man," she murmured.

"Well, I still don't trust him," Travis said, kicking dirt into the fire ring. "It's too unusual for him to just wander into our camp."

"Of course he didn't just happen in," she agreed. "He knew where we were. I have some ideas on that, but I'll keep them to myself for now. If it's any comfort, I don't trust him either. Still, we can use his help. The fight in Ama City will not be easy."

Wings flapped overhead. Zeldana landed a few yards away, excitement in her stride. "I've been to the Sun Bracil. They have word that Tark Lonan has surrendered to the aliens... without a fight. Lord Randoor has alerted all the bracils to prepare for an attack. Even now, my people are storing up rocks and bracing up the perimeters of our bracil."

"Surrendered without a fight," Cynara repeated. "Made a present to the aliens is more like it. Have you any word of Ama City, Zeldana?"

The bird shifted her wings in a gesture resembling a shrug. "No word has come to us about Ama City, Princess. However, my contact says Lord Randoor and a clatch of his guard are on their way there now."

"Then we must get there as soon as possible." Cynara touched Travis's arm. "Go see what progress Maltron's made with that transport."

"Of course." He sprinted uphill.

Zeldana hesitated, feathers puffing as if the words carried weight. "There is one more line from the Souuifan, Princess. I did not speak it before."

She recited softly:

"When the wounded falter, beware the hand that steadies them; For aid may mask a path that leads astray."

Cynara's eyes flicked toward Maltron's distant silhouette. The words struck too close, stirring unease.

"One more thing," Zeldana continued quickly, "my *bracil-diag* told me of an old healer in the Sun Mountains. If the Lady Cynara will stop there, she might find proper care for her hand. We think you'll need all your strength in Ama City."

Cynara hesitated. Her first impulse was to press straight on, but her hand was not healing and drained her strength. "You may be right, Zeldana. I'll make the stop if you show me exactly where it is and if it's not far out of our way."

"I will tell you now. And with your permission, I wish to return to my bracil, to help defend it with my people."

Cynara stared, caught off guard. "Of course. You may go. We will miss you. You've been of great service to me, and I shall not forget it. When this fight is over, and if I survive, please come to me, Zeldana."

"I will," the bird promised. She described the healer's route carefully, and Cynara listened. When finished, Zeldana spread her wings to launch.

"Are you going to say goodbye to Travis?" Cynara asked gently.

Zeldana's eyes reflected regret. "I should… but if I see his face, I may not leave. Will you tell him for me?"

Cynara nodded, watching as the bird ran awkwardly across the clearing, caught the wind, and lifted into the sky. She waved as Zeldana made a final pass before heading toward the higher peaks.

Let us go also, she told Linhok. The cat rose to join her as she started up the hill. The urgency to reach Ama City grew inside her like a tumor.

Chapter Eighteen

A Necessary Delay

MALTRON STEPPED INTO THE ROAD thirty yards ahead of the transport, waving his arms until the vehicle slowed and braked to a halt. He strode to the driver's window and shouted, "The Princess Cynara is injured and needs your transport. It's imperative she gets to Ama City at once."

The driver regarded him warily, eyes coursing up and down. "The Princess? I don't see any Princess. What would she be doing out here?"

"She's just over that hill. She was attacked on her way to Tark Lonan, and her skimmer was damaged. Turn this around while I fetch her."

The driver's reluctance was clear, and Maltron steeled himself to take the transport if necessary. Then the man's expression shifted as he gazed over Maltron's shoulder. Damon turned his head, spotting Cynara cresting the rise with Linhok at her side and Travis trailing behind.

"Yeah, I see the girl and that wild cat. You couldn't mistake her. You'll need to give me room to turn this," he said gruffly.

Maltron backed off as the driver maneuvered the transport. When Cynara approached, the man climbed down, bowed briefly, and said, "I will follow your wishes, Lady. But this delays my pick-up. Am I to be compensated?"

Cynara's smile was faint. "Of course—if there's anyone left to pay you. You're from Ama City?" A nod. "There may not be much left when we return. A war has begun."

The driver frowned. "Lady, I left only yesterday morning. There was no war—"

"There is now. I must return at once. My skimmer is unusable. Will you drive us, or shall my man?" She glanced toward Maltron.

"I prefer to protect my interests," the driver said firmly. "You can ride up front, Lady. Your companions will ride in back." His glance lingered on Linhok.

"That will be fine," Cynara replied. She sent Linhok to the trailer, then turned to her companions. "You will ride with him."

"As you wish," Maltron said, though he disliked leaving her unguarded. Travis's scowl suggested he felt the same. Yet, they had no other options.

WITHIN MINUTES THEY SQUEEZED into the trailer among boxes of merchandise. Linhok claimed a crate as his perch. Maltron found the light switch, sat against a box, and exhaled.

"Not even cozy grain sacks this time," Travis muttered. "And no Zeldana." His voice dipped. "She didn't even say goodbye."

"Maybe she had to hurry," Maltron said, pulling dice from his pocket. "You know duet?"

Travis looked up. "Of course."

Maltron grinned, tossed the hexagon dice, and laid down a credit.

"I don't have many credits," Travis admitted, though he matched the bet.

"Doesn't the Princess pay you well?" Maltron asked, watching the roll.

"She doesn't pay me anything. I volunteered."

"No pay? Why?"

"Because she's trying to save our planet. Were you always a mercenary?" Travis's stare was sharp.

Maltron licked his lip, uneasy at the accusation. "Yeah, pretty much. When you're on your own, the only things you have are yourself and your skills. I'm worth a lot."

"I have skills too," Travis said, rolling again. "But I donate them. If the aliens win, we have nothing."

Maltron shook the dice, considering. "Okay, I get it. But it doesn't put a roof over your head or food in your mouth."

Travis shrugged.

They finished the game in silence. Travis won when Maltron's last roll went over the limit. He stretched, leaned back. "Another round?"

Travis shook his head, positioning his pack as a pillow. Might as well get a few winks in while we have the chance." He laid down, dropping his head on the pack, and closed his eyes.

Maltron watched him settle, glanced at the feline, and decided neither seemed worried. Maybe sleep was best, though he couldn't relax. He gnawed on a strip of alphare and reflected on his life.

Like so many born on this planet, he'd seemed destined for a life of farming, a big, strong farm boy with just enough wits to carry on the life work of his family. Only he was smarter than that; he'd wanted more. At thirteen, he'd gone to the city with his cousin and found a whole new future. Loading jobs led to better work, special training, then mercenary pay.

Now those "special" skills might matter. But how much could they accomplish—a young mechanic, an injured sorceress, a fierce cat, and a hired killer? The last thought left a bitter taste. It was the truth of what he'd become, and not what he had ever intended.

UP FRONT, CYNARA STUDIED the driver. "Do you know these mountains well?"

"Ergin," he interrupted. "My name is Ergin. And yes, I know them pretty well. Been traveling them for many years."

"I need to make a stop, Ergin, at a place perhaps ten or fifteen miles along the road we'll be taking. Someone I must see is there."

Ergin's eyes drifted to her bandaged hand, and he nodded. "The healer, I'd guess."

"You know him?"

"Aye. Most who travel across these mountains do. You just relax, Lady, and I'll get you there."

The transport moved slowly but steadily through the mountains. Cynara shifted impatiently. *So much at stake—should I really take the time to see the healer?* She tested her injury, trying to grasp her vinte with swollen fingers. A sharp stab of pain assured her she must.

Frustrated, she eased her hand back to her lap. Most injuries she could self-heal, but broken bones were harder, and a compound fracture needed setting. She closed her eyes, focusing healing energy for a few minutes. Between the berry potion and her own skills, she kept the bleeding to a seep.

When the ache eased, she asked, "How were things when you left Ama City, Ergin? You said yesterday morning?"

The driver spared her a glance. "Yes, Lady. I left early, dropped off fruit at Harvest, then started over the mountains to Plainsford. Everything was calm, though busy. I noticed the old walls being worked on, officials scurrying. Come to think of it, more guards on the gates than usual. Looked like the city was being protected. What's happening, Lady?"

"Invasion," Cynara answered briefly. At least the governor and council had responded to her warning. But it wouldn't be enough. Without the protection screens, Ama City would fall quickly. *Are the aliens there now?* she wondered. Visions gave no sense of time—past, present, or future. What she'd seen may not happen for days yet or could be happening even now. She drew back from her own thoughts as she realized the driver was still speaking to her.

"—tell me. Are they from one of the other planets?"

"No, not within our sun's system. From another star—an alien race. I've seen them."

Ergin gaped, mouth open, then snapped it shut. "I asked." He said nothing more. Cynara didn't elaborate.

The turnoff to the healer's place came up on the right. Ergin pulled the transport off the highway. "The healer's back that way," he said, pointing up the narrow road. "About half a mile into the woods. I'll wait here."

Cynara nodded, climbed down, and found her companions emerging from the trailer. *I'll scout the way, my Lady,* Linhok informed her, padding ahead.

"I'll take Travis with me," she said, motioning him to her side. "Maltron, you stay behind with our driver." She knew he understood her implied instruction—make sure Ergin didn't leave. Not that she distrusted the man, but she could take no chances.

As she turned to the path, she caught Maltron leaning against the transport, fishing dice from his pocket. "How 'bout a game of duet?" he called, loud enough for her to hear.

A smile touched her lips as she started up the road. Then she froze. The sound of a supersonic engine approached. Ahead, Linhok bolted toward the forest.

Get off the road, my Lady. Approaching skyship.

Cynara tilted her head up, spotting the fast-moving scout ship tracking the road from Tark Lonan. "Follow me!" she shouted to Travis, dashing for the cover of the woods.

They crouched between bushes, not speaking as they heard the engine's roar overhead crescendo, diminishing as it continued to follow the road until it faded from their hearing. "Scouting," she murmured, straightening and gazing around the now-empty sky.

"There might be more," Travis warned, following her lead.

"We'll stay alert. Linhok is on the move." She resumed her trek, her hand rubbing gently against the bandaged one that now ached from the sudden movement. Travis fell into step beside her.

TRAVIS PACED THE SMALL ROOM, restless. In his mind, he reviewed everything that had happened in the past few days, right up to the unexpected appearance of Maltron. He didn't trust the mercenary. For all he knew, the man might have killed the transport driver and made off with his truck. Yet the princess had trusted him to make sure it was there when they returned. He paused to gaze at her.

Cynara sat nearby, her injured hand cradled in the healer's care, eyes half-closed as she began the slow breathing ritual that always preceded her trances. He knew the signs now—the way her shoulders eased, the way her gaze unfocused, the way silence seemed to thicken around her.

She'd refused the sleeping drought the healer offered to numb the pain while he reset the bones, preferring to use her own meditation to control it. Yet, Travis could see she was preparing again, despite the toll it took. He remembered how pale and trembling she had been after the last vision. *Is she stronger now, or simply forcing herself because necessity leaves her no choice?*

The healer, a man called Lambeth, worked steadily, packing her hand with poultices, moving the bone gingerly into place and securing it before closing the torn skin. All the while, he murmured instructions to his daughter. Travis barely noticed the girl until she stepped closer, arms folded, watching him with curiosity.

"There's no need to fret," she said. "My father knows what he's doing. Your friend is in good hands."

Travis shook his head quickly. "I wasn't worried about that. I can see she's safe. I was…thinking about other things."

The girl tilted her head, studying him. "Would you like to voice them? We can go out on the porch. She won't need you for a while."

Travis hesitated, then glanced back at Cynara. Her breathing had deepened, her body slackening as she slipped further into trance. He knew she was beyond hearing him now. With a sigh, he let the girl tug him toward the door.

Once outside, the girl introduced herself as Bethayne before looking back at the door. "The lady is your partner?"

"Great Tiel, no!" Travis almost shouted. Then he laughed. "You don't know who she is, do you? That's Princess Cynara." At the look on the girl's face, his grin broadened and he caught her hand sympathetically. "It's understandable. I didn't know her when I first met her either."

As the girl looked up to him, he was struck by her intense beauty with the deep brown eyes and hair of almost the same color that framed her small face. He pulled his hand away.

She blushed, then asked, "What were you thinking in there if not worry for her?"

With a sigh, Travis told her about his plans for the university and his concern for his family. He spoke cautiously, not mentioning Cynara's visions or the alien invasion. Soon enough the whole planet would know about it. He'd not spoil these moments of peace.

SMOKE AND DUST CLOUDS ERUPTED from Ama City as missiles struck. A dozen sky hoppers crisscrossed overhead, firing into the streets. Guards scrambled to return fire, but their weapons were no match for alien craft. Cynara's heart plunged. *Was this happening now—or a vision of the future?*

Panic set in as she watched helplessly in astral form. No Clan reinforcements appeared. Concentrating, she pulled back to her body. A sharp jerk, then her eyes snapped open. Linhok's alarm echoed in her mind as a hand touched her arm.

"I'm okay! I'm okay," she said quickly, though her voice trembled.

The healer leaned close, concern etched in his face. "Lady, perhaps you should lie down. You've forced yourself too far."

Cynara's breath came shallow, her limbs heavy. The trance had drained her more than she wanted to admit. She pressed her elbow to her knees, trying to steady herself. *It's worse each time,* she thought. *Or perhaps I'm simply learning to push harder, faster, because necessity leaves no choice.*

Another hand steadied her shoulder—gentle, reassuring. And in that instant, Zeldana's warning whispered back: *beware the hand that steadies them.*

Her turquoise eyes flicked toward the touch, unease stirring beneath her exhaustion.

"There isn't time," she whispered, voice strained. "Ama City is burning. I must get back."

"You should rest," the healer repeated gently. "You've done well—controlling the bleeding, holding infection at bay—but it has taken a toll. Your body shows it."

Cynara closed her eyes briefly, forcing her breathing to slow. She knew he was right. Her skin felt clammy, her head light. Yet urgency pressed harder than fatigue. "I can't rest. Every moment matters."

The healer offered her water, watching carefully. "Lady, I see a patient who is exhausted yet determined. If you must go, then at least tell me what troubles you."

Cynara hesitated, then spoke. She told him of the failing crops, the invasion forces, the Clan's faltering defenses, and the vision of Ama City under attack. The healer listened silently, nodding, his face grave.

"It is hard to convince people of danger when it is not yet visible," she concluded. "It's even more difficult to make them believe something is so dangerous that the Clan of Cantra can't protect them."

"But I believe you. I presume it's your intention to stop this invasion—just you and a man barely past childhood?"

"There are a few others." Cynara's lips were grim. "We must try. Some resources are available to me, possibly more on Corlan. However, I have to get to them. If we acquire a shuttle at the port, we can get there within two hours." She paused, casting a somber look at the healer.

He stood, poured two cups of osang, and handed one to Cynara. "Of course, you do. It's expected of one in your position, and you would not shirk any of your duties. I think somehow that all-knowing Clan has once again managed to provide a sorceress with the necessary talent and skill for the needs of the time. Have confidence in yourself and the Clan."

While they sipped and talked, the healer offered some advice. His counsel was practical, and as Cynara listened, a plan began to form. When she outlined it, he nodded. "Yes...yes, it might work. But with your height and fair skin, you're easily recognized. Bethayne can help transform you."

A short time later, Bethayne and Travis came back into the house, all smiles and murmured words. He spotted Cynara and his whole demeanor changed. "You're awake. I'm sorry I was –"

"Out for a walk," she completed. "It's okay. I needed to recover from that excursion and Lambeth has helped me come up with a plan."

Lambeth nodded at Travis. "I understand what lies ahead. If you are to face this, you should not do it alone. My daughter knows some healing, and she is resourceful. If she is willing, take her with you."

Bethayne's chin lifted. "It's my duty. I want to help."

Cynara gave a weary smile. "Then let us prepare."

Bethayne was eager. Travis objected, but Cynara cut him off. "Sooner or later, it will be her battle. We could use her help now."

The healer beamed. "Then it is settled."

After they explained the first step, Bethayne fingered Cynara's silky hair. "It's finer than Araman hair. Are you sure?"

"It's necessary," Cynara said. She turned to Travis. "Linhok may have caught dinner. Find him and prepare it."

Travis bowed mockingly. "Certainly, My Lady."

Lambeth excused himself. Cynara touched her hair. "Drastic, but our best hope. Let's do it."

Bethayne grinned. "It'll be a whole new you!" She reached for the scissors.

THE SMALL PARTY RETURNED toward the pass looking like farmers; two tall lads in tunics and breeches, and a small dark girl in work skirts. On close inspection, one might recognize the Princess of Corlan in the shorter boy. Her hair was cropped close in Araman fashion, now golden brown from Bethayne's herbal concoction. Linhok paralleled them, unseen.

Although she wore a cap with a bill shadowing her face, Cynara practiced squinting, trying to hide her turquoise eyes. The disguise would suffice in Ama City, where few knew her face. While she could cast an illusion spell to alter the color, maintaining it was draining.

"Princess, I must talk to you privately," Travis whispered.

Cynara glanced at Bethayne. Travis shook his head. "I don't want her to hear."

"Bethayne, please gather a few handfuls of nuts and berries for rations," Cynara said.

Bethayne nodded, though her expression showed she wasn't fooled. As she started to bow, Cynara stopped her. "That's not necessary—and dangerous. From now on, I am Kartha, a farmer like you."

They agreed. When Bethayne was gone, Travis spoke low. "Kartha, I think Maltron is an enemy. He showed up right after your ambush, knew where to find us, and had a cut on his face where you scratched your attacker. It all fits."

Cynara laughed. "Do you think I don't know? Of course it was Maltron. Linhok and I suspected but couldn't place him at first."

"But—?"

"Isn't it safer to keep your enemies close? He may have truth to share—or a falling out with his allies. At the least, he has seen the aliens and knows their technology. When I need that, I can get it."

Her tone chilled Travis, and he shivered.

"Let's use this time to gather food," she said. "It may prove our salvation."

MALTRON GREW RESTLESS. The Princess expected him to wait, though he'd have preferred to join her. Ergin seemed content in the sunshine. Apart from the alien flyover, the wait was uneventful. They played duet and buster, but boredom set in. Maltron scouted the perimeter, found little, and wondered if Cynara and Travis would return at all. "A quick stop at the healer's," she'd said. Hours had passed; the sky was darkening.

Then Linhok bounded from the woods, followed by three figures. At first Maltron saw only two lads and a girl. Then recognition dawned, the gait of the Princess. He strode forward, smiling.

"I almost didn't recognize you," he said.

"That's the idea," Cynara replied. She gestured to Bethayne. "This is Bethayne. I am Kartha now. I intend to slip into Ama City undetected. If any of you disclose my cover, you will regret it—for the short span of life you have left. Now, let's move. I want to be at Ama City by sunrise."

Chapter Nineteen

Whispers Beneath the Walls

THE SUN WAS JUST BEGINNING to rise when the transport pulled to the side of the road to disgorge its weary group of passengers at the edge of Ama City. Payment marker in hand, the driver turned the vehicle around to retrace the road toward the mountains. Even though they'd tried to rest, the ride had been too uneven to really sleep deeply. The only one even partially refreshed was Linhok.

Cynara scratched the cat's ears and gazed thoughtfully at the city. We must part now, my friend. If you are seen, many people will know I am near. You know my plans. Meet us this evening at the spaceport, where your help will be needed.

Agreed, yet I fear for you, Lady. Take care and trust no one. Linhok nudged her shoulder once, then was gone, disappearing into the shadows of the walled city where he could move unseen through the passages.

She turned to the rest of her companions. "Now, it's our turn. There will be guards at the gates. I don't want anyone to know I'm here. The easiest way to avoid anyone is to follow the old maze into the city. Everyone needs to stay close behind me and no talking. These walls amplify sounds easily, and it could be a problem if anyone is patrolling them."

Entering the computer key to the access door, she slipped into one of the maze gates of the outer wall, followed closely by Bethayne, then Travis with Maltron guarding the rear. She noticed the latter brandished the gun Travis returned to him, holding it ready if needed. The weight of his presence directly behind her sent a prickle of unease across her skin.

After a few yards, the tunnels became dark with only slight illumination from the occasional breaks to the sky. They skulked inside the same walls Cynara had taken her skimmer careening through only a few days before. Like the maze they formed, the inner tunnels were equally challenging to navigate, and Cynara relied heavily on her seeker sense to guide her.

Again, ancient voices cried to her from the walls, anxious to tell their stories. This time, she found it harder to ignore them, especially when she had to touch the walls occasionally for guidance. "I know I promised to come and listen," she murmured softly, "but now is not the time."

Despite her efforts to close the voices out, one broke through her screening, a life memory so strong it could not be ignored. She stopped dead still and listened while it swiftly impressed its whole existence on her. She caught her breath sharply: it was an old mind and what it conveyed surprised her yet did not.

At Cynara's intake of breath, Travis moved past Bethayne to whisper urgently, "Is anything wrong? Are you all right?"

She nodded sharply, her face an unreadable mask in the darkness, then signaled for silence. Taking a deep breath, she focused again on her destination and raised mental screens against the voices. It was difficult enough to follow her seeker sense without the screens, but with them up, she had to concentrate fully on the destination she'd chosen. She'd used her temple to Tiel as a focus point, knowing she had a strong imprint in its alcove—probably stronger than anywhere else on the entire planet—and that it was safe and undisturbed behind the security screens surrounding her apartments.

She paused at a T-intersection in the maze, closed her eyes in concentration, discerned the route, then frowned. It required crossing an area directly under one of the grids to the sky, and she could hear voices above them talking. She motioned to her companions to follow her one at a time and quietly, then flattened herself against the wall on the opposite side of the slanting ray of light and eased slowly and carefully across.

Briefly, she glimpsed one of the men above her, a small dark man, slimly built with yellow-toned skin—one of the aliens. So, her far sense had been correct, and the aliens already were in Ama City.

Behind her, Bethayne quickly traversed the area, moving easily and gracefully. Travis followed, but when he completed the final steps, he bumped against a projection of stone from the wall, and the sound of the scuff echoed down the tunnel. In a heartbeat, Cynara grabbed his arm and yanked him far into the darkness. Maltron ducked back into the T-corridor, out of sight.

A face peered through the grid into the tunnels, then a flashlight's beam cut into the darkness on each side. The small group was far enough back to avoid the illumination, yet close enough to see the details of the face. Cynara glimpsed Bethayne's eyes widen, the fear plain in them, but the girl held herself still and silent. Cynara marked the restraint with approval.

The alien said something in his language to the other, his companion responded, then both laughed and moved away. Try as she may, Cynara could not read their thoughts, although she'd made a desperate effort to determine if they suspected anything. They couldn't enter the maze without the computer keys, but they could be waiting at the exits. When Maltron appeared from the corner, she flicked her uninjured hand, urging him to cross.

He quickly moved, crossing silently to join everyone, then urged them on with quick gestures. Cynara caught his arm and pulled him ahead a few feet with her. In a shallow voice, she said, "I couldn't understand what they said. Could you?"

"I don't understand them either. Why would you think–?"

"Be honest. You're either with us, or you're not." Her voice was soft, but her words conveyed her message. Time to declare your position.

He hesitated before answering. "I don't know many words, but it seemed like the one guy told the other it was an animal of some kind."

"If you're lying to me, and we walk into an ambush, I'll cut your throat before I die."

His head jerked down in a nod. "I'll explain more when we're out of these tunnels."

"Yes, you will. Take point. They can see you first." She dropped back to Bethayne, tapped her hand, and they resumed the journey. Although they encountered three more openings, they had no problems with watchers above and crossed them unseen.

After what felt like hours but was scarcely more than one, they arrived at the gate Cynara wanted and stepped through the door into a stairwell filled with shadows from the tall building next to the maze. Weapon readied, Maltron led the way up, with Cynara following closely. Her vinte was in her hand, but no one looked their way while the sound of munitions in other parts of the city drew everyone's attention. She could smell the dust and gunpowder in the air. Stiffening with fury at the damage to her city, she hurried her companions through the alley to the end, where they stopped long enough for her to evaluate the city's status. They'd reached the most dangerous part. If citizens weren't freely moving within, getting to the palace would be challenging or impossible.

Ahead of them lay about two hundred yards of open streets to cover to reach the palace, then they had to get through the inside corridors to reach her quarters. Cynara had a plan, assuming she could gain access to the passages within the palace, but it would depend on the situation inside.

She edged her way to the corner and gazed out toward the main streets. Ama City bustled with aliens, dozens of them in the immediate area, and skimmers passing across the city on frequent patrols. To her relief, she also spotted citizens going about their daily business unimpeded by the alien invaders. The people looked scared, scurrying through the streets and the market square like they expected more bombing at any moment. Along the way, the invaders patrolled, weapons in their hands to ensure everyone stayed in line.

She turned back to Maltron. "Put your gun out of sight. If there's anything we need to know about these aliens, now is the time to tell us."

"Most of them don't speak our language, so we shouldn't be stopped by them. Cy—" He caught himself and corrected. "Kartha, I worked for Governor Haburn, not the aliens. When they arrived, they contacted Haburn. He assigned my duties. I worked with a couple of different ones, but I couldn't tell one from another. I have seen the Empress; I don't think she knows me. They're a cold-blooded lot. If I hadn't left them, I would be dead now for failure to bring you in."

She nodded. "So Haburn was in league with them, making it that much easier for them to come in. I suspected as much, but I had hoped otherwise. And the first city under occupation is Tark Lonan, handed over without a fight." She looked at the damaged walls of her capital. "At least Ama City fought."

She took a deep breath and turned to Bethayne and Travis. "We're a family come to town to find work. Our farm is destroyed by the foul water and can no longer support us. We left our parents there. Maltron, you and Bethayne are to be married. Travis and I are her brothers. Let's hope we don't get stopped."

They moved from behind one building into the doorway of the next one, where they paused to see if anyone had noticed the dash to cover. Everything still seemed calm, so they stepped out onto the street, moving naturally as if they'd just come from the building. Like any other strangers in the city, they banded close together and looked around in wonder. Bethayne and Travis stared wide-eyed, their wonder plain enough that Cynara doubted they could have feigned it.

Undisturbed, they made their way down the street, continuing to the right toward the government sector. A skimmer cut in front of them, nearly knocking them over, and stopped in front of the council hall. A small alien woman, clad in ornamental armor and an elaborate headdress, stepped from the craft.

"The Empress," Maltron whispered into Cynara's ear.

She nodded once in acknowledgment and continued toward the Palace. One of the aliens stepped up to her and muttered something unintelligible at them. Cynara glanced at Maltron in puzzlement, then shrugged.

"We don't understand you," Travis said.

The alien scowled. "Pa-pers."

"What?" Maltron spoke this time.

"Pa-pers," he repeated.

Maltron shook his head. "I'm sorry. We don't understand." From behind her, he nudged Cynara to continue, put his arm protectively around Bethayne, and started forward again.

They were almost at the Palace entrance when the alien caught up with them again, this time with another one in tow. The second alien spoke Araman. "Hold. We need to see your papers."

"We just got to the city today," Maltron said. "I don't have my papers on me; I left them at the lodge."

The alien eyed them suspiciously, his hand hovering near his weapon. "Were you not told to carry them with you when they were issued?"

Chapter Twenty

Breaking Into The Palace

DAMON FEIGNED SURPRISE. "Why, no. I figured everyone in the city had them, so we left 'em at our lodging."

"We will go get them." The alien motioned with his weapon to point back in the direction they'd come.

"All right," he agreed, "but I will leave my woman and her brothers here. No need for all of us to go." Maltron figured that if he could get this one away from the rest, he could take care of him in an alley while the others got into the palace.

"We all go," the alien said, then spoke to his companion in their language.

Maltron sighed, looking meaningfully at Cynara. Her hand already moved toward her boot where the vinte waited; Maltron's own blade was concealed in a sleeve sheath. At her almost imperceptible nod, Maltron shoved Bethayne away from him, flipped the knife into his hand, and drove it up into the rib cage of the alien who'd spoken. At the same time, Cynara went into action, pulling the vinte from her boot and flicking it into the chest of the other.

Travis grabbed Bethayne's arm and began pulling her in a run toward the Palace entrance.

“To the left,” Cynara yelled after them, lunged to retrieve her vinte, stooped low, and ran toward the Palace.

Just inside the entry was a passage to the left, and three more of the aliens came at them from the town. “Go on,” Maltron urged as a blast of fire from one of their weapons blazed over her head. He hit the floor and rolled into the side passage. As he came up again, his own laser gun was in his hand, and he got off a return shot at the nearest alien. The man dropped, screaming in agony as the blast burned into his leg. Maltron aimed again for the second one and fired a moment before one of the alien flares hit his shoulder.

He rocked back into the passage, managed somehow to hang onto his weapon, and fired yet another blast. He rolled to his feet and ran, bumping against walls as he went. His shoulder sagged, numb from the strike, but he kept moving.

The passage curved, and he followed it along, crouched low and running as fast as he could. He could hear pursuit behind him, pointed the gun back, and fired, knowing at best the blast would hit a wall. Still, it might slow them.

Ahead, Travis stepped out into the corridor, intercepted him, and shoved him into a side alcove where Cynara knelt working a lock puzzle to open the concealed door. When she eased the last piece into place, a section of the back wall raised enough for them to slide underneath. Travis pushed Maltron through, followed him, and Bethayne slid in barely in front of Cynara, who pressed the button on the puzzle's reverse side moments before an alien reached the alcove. Once the button was pushed, the puzzle on the other side scrambled again, locking the door in place.

Cynara reached along the wall near the button, found the torch concealed there, and flipped the beam on. Then she was on her feet and heading down a corridor to the right. "Come on, we haven't got a lot of time. They'll be trying to break through the wall."

As he got to his feet, Damon staggered, the sharp ache in his shoulder replacing the numbness. He stumbled after the others. Bethayne watched him for a moment, then dropped back to offer support. "You're hurt," she stated bluntly.

He nodded. "Shoulder—just starting to hurt."

"Hang on. I'll take care of it when we get inside."

The corridor led them up two levels and about fifty yards back before they stopped outside a pulsing purple energy screen.

Maltron leaned against the wall as Cynara stepped in front of it. Cynara shifted her weapon smoothly to her left hand, her movements as precise as ever.

"Now what?" Travis asked, hovering behind her but glancing backward often for any sign of pursuit.

Cynara waved him to silence and keyed a number sequence into the computer link on her wrist. She punched the last number, said, "Hurry," then ran into the field, which disappeared just before she hit it. Bethayne and Maltron followed, with Travis barely through before it blazed back on again.

Cynara relaxed, pressed another button on this side of the wall, and waited as a section slid aside, allowing them to enter her chambers. The others followed her in, Maltron now breathing heavily as the full impact from his wound hit. The Princess glanced back, pointed to her bedchamber.

"Take him in there, Bethayne, and do what you can for him. Travis, there's food and drink in the pantry. Please fix us something while I contact Corlan."

EMPRESS Y'RIEL PACED THE corridor just outside the royal chambers. The pulsing purple field cast an eerie glow on everything in the area and taunted the Heliotian queen. The guard she'd stationed outside Cynara's chambers hadn't been quick enough. When the field had gone off, he'd hesitated, called for instructions, then stepped into the doorway just as the screen came back on. He was sliced in half. The remains on this side had already been cleaned up. She imagined the other half still fouling the chamber beyond.

"There is no more to be seen here, Y'Tauk. The guard reported the field down, stepped into it, and it came back on again. I want to interview the guards from the palace entrance about the group of locals they encountered. I think they might be tied to this."

Y'Tauk fell in a pace behind her, as was his place. "As you wish, Highness. I'll bring them to you in the main hall if that suits your Highness."

"That will be fine. And ask Y'Van to be in attendance. I'll expect them in ten minutes." She paused, turned to face Y'Tauk. "You may go now."

With a respectful bow, her man hastened to his task. He would not risk the wrath of his queen. Y'riel watched him leave, pondering the significance of what had happened. First, a group of four "travelers" had come into the city, stabbed and killed two soldiers—this much they knew from one who had died reporting it. Then they entered the palace, killing another and injuring one, escaped down a side corridor, and disappeared behind a wall. Then the unfortunate guard at the main entrance to the royal chambers reported the force field was off. When he started to enter, it came back on, killing him. Who had turned the force field off? Was it Princess Cynara herself, or did one of these uncooperative local officials know how to do it after all?

The two surviving guards from the Palace entrance approached cautiously. They had failed to guard her property, and Y'riel knew they were apprehensive about this summons. Y'Van arrived behind her and stepped to her side. The guards lowered their eyes at the sight of Y'Van the Equalizer. She smiled grimly, knowing his presence did nothing to calm their fears.

"Y'Staun and Y'Baln, come forward at the command of Her Highness." The order came from Y'Tauk the Voice, and they obeyed immediately, falling to their knees and prostrating themselves before their ruler.

"Rise, humbled servants," the queen commanded. "You will serve me now with information. It is my desire to know all you can remember about these creatures who infiltrated the Palace. How many were they, and how did they appear?"

Nervously, Y'Staun responded. "There were four of them, Highness. Three males and one female crum of this world. One male was bigger than the others, maybe more mature. The other two males were of a smaller build, similar to my own. The female was small, a little shorter than your Highness."

"Describe the female in detail, how she looked and behaved."

"She had dark brown hair, below the shoulders and tied back with a cord. Her clothes were like the rest of the farmer-scum here. She appeared frightened and followed quickly after one of the smaller males when they broke into the palace."

The description did not fit the Princess—unless she could use her alleged sorcery to change her appearance. From all reports, the Princess was tall for a woman, and her hair was almost as white as the glistening sands of Helios. Y'riel's brow wrinkled, the only outward sign of a frown. "Tell me again, exactly what happened?"

She listened intently as they repeated their story of the break into the Palace. She turned to Y'Van when they finished. "Have you put a crew to work smashing through the wall in that alcove?"

"Yes, Highness. The puzzle lock is intricate and well-constructed. We tried first to break through there but have abandoned it to enter through the wall itself. We are partially through."

She nodded. "Good work, although I doubt getting through the wall will help us. Whoever they were, they are probably safely behind that force field. If it was not the Princess who entered, then it was someone who knows the Palace, the puzzle locks, and the code to the force field."

"Agreed, Highness," Y'Van stated. "However, if we have guards stationed outside the chambers and at the location of the force field within the walls, they will not leave the chambers either."

She nodded thoughtfully. "Very well. Place a triate guard at each location. If the field goes off again, instruct each man to move quickly to the other side. If four of them have to get through, then it should allow time for three to get through as well."

"Done, Highness," Y'Van acknowledged. "And what would your Highness like me to do about these failures?"

She lowered her eyes at the two men before her. Back on Helios, she would not hesitate, but here she might need them. "Nothing—for now. Dismiss them, Y'Tauk."

After they'd gone, Empress Y'riel the Provider, exalted queen and unquestioned leader of the Heliotian star system, closed her eyes and meditated. So far, this invasion was successful—too successful. Ama City had resisted for several sun markers—the equivalent of twelve Araman hours—but had surrendered quickly enough when Heliotian weapons proved superior.

The sniveling governor had opened the palace himself, anxious only to remain alive and with the building intact. While he'd disengaged several protective force fields, he claimed he had no code for the one around the Princess's chamber. Only the Princess knew it, he'd said.

Her experts had studied the field and found it very powerful, unlike others in the city. They could find no way to disengage it, and they could not locate the source of the power that maintained it. When questioned, Governor Rondu only stated Corlan powered it and babbled something about Clan coming to their aid soon.

Perhaps, Y'riel mused, the small purple-blue planet should be her next target. If they had any powerful weapons, they had not displayed them.

Chapter Twenty-One

Recovery and the Next Step

Cynara stared at an interactive strategic map of Arama, noting the damaged areas across the planet. While not as bad as she'd feared, the attacks still alarmed her. Tark Lonan and Ama City showed occupation and armed control by significant numbers of alien forces. Along the west coast of the main continent, ten small villages appeared to be taken as well. Thus far, Weilock Center remained undisturbed, and reports from there indicated their defense shields were operative and in good condition. Tark Noter to the east and Tark Sothin in the South Greens, as well as most of the port towns, were undisturbed as yet, but their defense shields were in place. Cynara's messages included an apology from the governor of Iso Port for "doubting her judgment."

A lot of good that does. At least the council members were taking her seriously now. She composed her thoughts to transmit her plans to Corlan, then concentrated. As the map flashed off, a blue sending screen replaced it. She focused on it and began her telepathic transmission, allowing her eyelids to lower again as she slipped into a light trance.

When Cynara opened her eyes again, she found a cup of steaming osang and a plate of hot spiced meats sitting on the table beside her. Grateful for the repast, she ate while she waited for a response from Corlan. It would take the Clan some time to analyze her transmission and make a decision. She knew how things worked on Corlan, and she realized the elders would not be receptive to her proposal. They had done nothing to stop or even deal with it.

From the other room, Maltron grunted in pain, and Cynara rose to see how he was doing. Bethayne sat next to him on the divan and applied a green salve to the nasty-looking burn on his shoulder. His tunic was off, allowing Cynara to notice his broad shoulders and the sculpted definition of his chest muscles. A powerfully built man, she conceded. But not impervious to pain. He bit at his lip to avoid crying out and gripped the edge of the bed. She moved beside him, reaching out with her uninjured hand to clasp his where he white-knuckled the bed. He resisted a moment, then clung tightly to hers.

"Relax," she said in a gentle tone. Meeting Maltron's eyes, she concentrated her energy as her voice continued in a soothing drone. "Do not panic, but let my mind enter yours, and I will ease the pain. Now, close your eyes and picture the seas with their smooth, calm surface, gentle waves rolling the waters. Watch as the seabirds fly over and cast yourself up with them. Now, follow the birds; let them carry your pain out over the sea. As the birds go further away, the pain diminishes until it is finally gone—transferred with the birds, and you no longer feel it. Sleep now and heal."

Maltron's eyes fluttered shut, his hand slipping from the bed's edge and his body relaxing into natural sleep.

As Cynara released his hand, Zeldana's prophecy stirred again: *When the wounded falter…* She looked at Maltron, Bethayne, and Travis. Each faltered in their own way, and she was the one expected to steady them. Yet the warning whispered that even this role carried danger—that the act of steadying could itself lead astray.

Bethayne stared at her. "In Tiel's name, how did you do that?"

She laughed softly. "Some call it sorcery, but it's a mind trick I learned as a child. My mind is quite powerful, and it's not difficult to gain control of his."

The girl continued to stare at her as if she were some sort of demon, and as Cynara turned away, she found Travis watching her, a frown creasing his brow. *Oh, not you, too,* she thought.

But his question bore no connection to Bethayne's expression. "How bad off is Arama? I saw you studying the map."

"It's not as bad as I'd feared," she admitted, then told him the extent of the occupation.

"My family's land," Travis said, his own fears confirmed. "My father might have resisted. I hope none of them were hurt or killed. Is there any way to know?"

"We can't risk any communications with them. I'm sorry, Travis, but I hope they're all right." She nodded at Maltron. "We all ought to try to get some sleep. We have a long and difficult night ahead of us."

As she spoke, Cynara thought of the council's sudden apologies and the governor's cowardly surrender. Hands that claimed to steady Arama had already led it astray. *Beware the hand that steadies them,* Zeldana's warning whispered again, reminding her that false allies could be as dangerous as open enemies.

WHEN CORLAN FINALLY CALLED BACK, the spokesman for the Clan of Cantra expressed dismay over such a risky maneuver. He suggested that perhaps some other alternative might be less hazardous. When she asked for suggestions, the ideas proved limited and unimaginative. Staying in her apartments, pinned in by her own force field, was not an idea that Cynara liked and no other location on the planet offered more safety.

"On Corlan," she pointed out, "we possess more monitoring devices and more Minoan ships. Not to mention the full resources of the Clan of Cantra. I expect you will be able to support our defense efforts, will you not?"

"Of course, the Clan will assist in any way possible. It's just this option places you in great danger."

"As if I'm not in it already? Isn't this why I am the protector?"

He sputtered over his response, trying to formulate an objection, then signed off to discuss it with the clan leaders again. Cynara gazed at the blank screen in consternation. Where was the support she hoped to have? The Clan was not all-powerful; she knew as much. But she also understood they had some degree of power and some weapons, although they hadn't been used in centuries.

At length, Corlan agreed to her plan even though they considered it high risk. After signing off, Cynara looked around her communications alcove, regretting its loss. While it had been quite useful to her, she couldn't allow any of it to fall into the aliens' hands. It would have to be destroyed along with the private little temple.

Sighing, she closed down her screen and turned to the bedchamber. As she walked, the faint murmur of the walls returned to her mind—the same voices she'd heard in the maze. They spoke of welcome, of strangers once received in friendship. Zeldana's prophecy echoed: *strangers will come twice, one offering friendship, one bringing death.* Perhaps the walls themselves bore witness to that first arrival. If so, then the prophecy was not only a warning for the future—it was a memory of the past.

Bethayne slept on the sitting couch, and Travis sprawled on the floor. There was plenty of room next to Maltron, and he would not wake until she told him, so she stretched out beside him and, setting her mental alarm, drifted off to sleep.

CYNARA MOVED SWIFTLY AROUND her chambers, securing what she could of her personal items in several of the hidden vaults in the room. She'd always suspected it would be handy to know where they all were, but she could never have predicted she'd need them for this purpose. No one could have, she reflected bitterly. Not even the Clan of Cantra, with all their mind power, could have predicted this.

She stopped, holding one of her loren gem tiaras, the one presented to her when she turned thirteen. She wanted to pack away all the valuable jewels so the aliens couldn't get to any of them. On the thought, she turned to the others. "Bethayne, please grab a cloth bag and place all the items from the Temple in them." She pointed to her personal alcove.

The girl bobbed her head, then hurried to comply.

Across the room, she noticed Travis occupied himself by going through the small but well-stocked pantry locating non-perishable food items. At the same time, Maltron worked the stiffness out of his shoulder. "It's nearly healed already," he said with a touch of surprise in his voice. "You have impressive magic, your Highness."

In another half-hour, they'd packed everything they were taking and stowed as many valuable items in the vaults as possible. They allowed another ten minutes to eat a small meal of hot meat rolls and osang to fortify them before starting their escape.

Although the others talked quietly, Cynara ate in silence, her thoughts returning to Linhok's report. It would not be easy, but she didn't think they had an alternative. Her gaze lingered on each of her companions, evaluating them as she went. Travis, young but loyal to her—he would die defending her if need be. She'd have to ensure he didn't. Maltron, still a bit of an unknown, but she trusted her instincts about him. Before he'd told her, she'd known he'd been one of her attackers, yet she trusted him to stand beside her. Bethayne, a young girl who was here for what reason? Travis? She seemed to have some attraction to him, but was it enough for her to continue risking her life? Would she panic at the wrong moment?

The prophecy's first words stirred faintly: strangers will come twice, one offering friendship, one bringing death. Bethayne's healing hands might be the friendship the walls remembered—but friendship could falter, and Cynara could not afford to trust blindly.

She finished her osang, thumped the cup down deliberately hard to get their attention, then spoke. "To each of you, I ask you to make a decision. We will leave soon, and what I'm proposing will not be easy. I do not hold any of you to stay with me. Ahead, our path will be dangerous, and we may not survive. I cannot ask this in blind obedience to me as Princess, so I ask you now to decide if you will go with me or make your own way to the possible safety of the shores." Hands folded on the table, she waited for their answers.

With barely a moment's pause, Travis spoke first, as she knew he would. "I'm going with you, Lady. I've come this far, and I will not desert you now."

Bethayne stared at the floor, wet her lips nervously, and glanced toward Travis. Cynara could guess her thoughts as she weighed her options. She could leave now, make her way back to her father, and maybe live out her life untouched there, but life wouldn't be the same. "I will go," she said softly.

"Thank you. Your skills might be needed," Cynara responded, pleased to have the young healer along. She turned her attention to Maltron. "And you, Damon?"

"I'm the hired help, remember? That's what you're paying me to do." He was not sarcastic, just straightforward.

"I release you from that obligation, and you may take anything you find in this room for your salary to this point. I will not have you sacrifice yourself because you were hired."

His eyes met hers, a flash of determination in them. "Then I choose to go with you. I may be a mercenary, but I know my chances are *redorfan* poor on this planet with the Heliotians in control."

Her lips twitched at the reference to the fate of the most harvested food fish on the planet. With a deep breath, Cynara rose to her feet. "Then, I thank all of you. Let's gather what we're taking—it is time to go."

While the others got their packs ready, Cynara retreated to her communications center.

Her fingers lingered over the unit regretfully, then she set a timer unit on it. In the alcove, she set another timer, then turned away. The walls had whispered of welcomes long past, of strangers once received in friendship. She wondered if destroying her temple meant silencing those voices forever—or if they would keep speaking, reminding her that friendship had once been real, before betrayal followed.

"We have to go now. Follow me quickly. We don't have much time."

She touched a panel behind the right side of her bed, and it slid aside, revealing a different passage from the one through which they'd entered. After the last one had stepped past, she closed it again, heard the lock click, then she led the way to the right in the darkness.

"How many of these secret passages are there?" Travis asked in a loud whisper.

"The city is riddled with them. Ama City has had many enemies to defend against over the centuries. Times were not always as peaceful as we've known them. I don't know all of the passages in the palace, but it's a foolish person who is unaware of all the exits from her own room."

They went down at a slight decline. "Feels like we've descended fifteen feet or more from your chambers," Maltron stated. "And we're going northeast."

"Good estimate," Cynara said as she spotted the faint glow from another pulsating force shield. She urged her team on and punched a code into her wrist computer. "It's going to be close," she muttered. "Hurry. If we're not out before the computer blows, we might be trapped here."

The field winked out, and they ran through it. Bethayne tripped and nearly fell, but Travis yanked on her arm, pulling her the rest of the way just as the purple field glowed to life again. Cynara breathed a little easier, then glanced at her computer link. It was dark and unresponsive.

"Well, they won't find anything in my chambers now, and they may be stuck in there a long time. I hope several of them got through." She turned to retake the lead. Now she could contact Linhok to let him know they were on their way.

THEY EXITED SEVERAL MILES from the palace near Ama City's outside walls. They paused to survey the scene beyond the passage then, satisfied that all was calm, crept through the dark city. Never had Cynara seen the capital city without some illumination, but no stores or lamps glowed under the occupation.

"We're not far from the spaceport," Cynara said softly. Through the gaps between the buildings, glimpses of the great ships' upward pointing nosecones and navigation turrets enticed them.

Cynara halted the little party at the edge of the spaceport and motioned them down in the shadows of the buildings.

"What now?" Travis whispered as he slipped up next to the Princess.

"We wait."

"Here? In plain sight?" His eyes widened in disbelief.

"The shadows will hide us well enough, and we don't have long to wait. Come on." She motioned with her head for him to follow her back into one of the dark corners formed by the structures. Although the sky was completely dark, the pale light from Corlan cast enough illumination to create wells of shadows and allowed them to see clearly.

"Looks like about thirty or so ships out there," Damon commented in a low undertone. "Can you fly any of them?"

"Possibly. At least well enough to get us off the ground and pointed toward Corlan."

"And then what?" Damon prompted.

"Then all we have to do is land it."

"Which you haven't done."

"Which I haven't done," she confirmed.

"Terrific," he said with a mirthless laugh.

"Can you do better?" Cynara asked, sudden anger coloring her tone.

"No. It's not an area I was trained in. And I didn't mean anything by it. I'm grateful you know anything about it. Truce?"

She nodded.

"Now, all we have to do is figure out how to get one and get away with it," Maltron mused.

Chapter Twenty-Two

Exit Plan

ONCE THEY SETTLED AND Cynara felt secure, she contacted Linhok, letting him know their location. Maltron listened as the leopard's progress came through her link, the princess narrating what she saw. He pictured the cat slipping through the low bushes surrounding the spaceport, hugging crates for cover. When she broke the connection, Maltron knew Linhok would handle the rest in his own way.

Within fifteen minutes, the leopard padded into their hiding place. Bethayne gasped, too loud, and Cynara shot her a sharp glance. Maltron froze, waiting to see if anyone had heard. No one came, and the girl mouthed an apology before retreating behind a crate.

For over half an hour, Maltron crouched beside Cynara, watching the activity at the spaceport. "We'll have to do something soon, or they'll discover the guards are missing," she whispered. She pointed across his vision. "That Firehawk model over there—I could fly it. If we can just get to it and get launched without interference."

Maltron studied the sleek ship, but his response was grim. “That won’t be easy. As soon as we fire the engines, the tower will request information. If we don’t respond, we’ll never get into the air.”

“Unless we take care of the tower somehow.”

Travis leaned forward. “There’s sure to be guards near it.”

“Not that many,” Cynara answered. “Linhok’s already explored around the tower. Six guards outside, a couple inside, and a crew of three.”

Travis’s jaw dropped. “Bethayne can’t take on a guard,” he objected.

Bethayne shot forward, frowning. “Don’t speak for me, Travis. I’ll do my part. I’m not disturbed at the idea of smacking one of those aliens on the head.”

Maltron raised his brows, impressed at her spirit. Cynara’s lips curved in amusement, but before she could speak, Maltron nudged her arm and pointed. “We may not have to worry about the tower. Look.”

A shuttle wheeled out toward the boarding terminal. Cynara whispered, “We’ll have to move quickly.”

She sprang to her feet, running crouched through the bushes. Maltron followed close behind, Travis and Bethayne lagging. Linhok moved ahead, clearing the path.

Within minutes, they were a dozen yards from the ship. Fuel hoses pumped into its tanks while technicians swarmed over the vessel. Cynara studied the scene, then signaled Linhok. Maltron watched her follow the leopard to a fallen guard. She stripped the uniform quickly, wincing as she tugged the sleeve over her injured hand. The fit was snug, but she pulled the cap low and strode toward the hangar.

Maltron held his breath as she blended with the workers. She moved confidently, but he caught the stiffness in her grip when she carried the tool bag. A moment later, she tossed it into the bushes near them and walked casually back toward the shuttle.

Travis muttered, “I wonder what the bag is.”

Maltron kept his voice low. “We’ll know soon enough. Linhok’s bringing it.”

The leopard appeared, dropping the bag at Travis’s feet. Inside were heavy maintenance suits. Maltron pulled one on, adjusting the fit. “Well, it appears we’ve been promoted,” Travis said with a grin.

The trio eased out of the shadows, moving toward the shuttle. Damon lifted a fuel line, carrying it as if it were his task. Cynara met them near the ramp, her eyes sharp. She directed Travis and Bethayne toward the pressurization controls, whispering for them to find a hiding place.

Both of them saw the alien approaching the loader, but Cynara quickened her pace to get there before him. She jumped into the open compartment and fired up the transport's engine just as he came even on the other side. The controls resisted at first, a warning light blinking red across the panel. She cursed under her breath, slammed the override, and the loader lurched forward with a grinding protest.

The alien barked something in his own tongue, eyes narrowing. He strode closer, puffing his shoulders to add height.

"This is my job," Cynara said, forcing her voice low and clipped. She tapped the maintenance logo on her uniform. "My responsibility to drive this thing. You understand?"

The alien shook his head violently. "No! I must do it. Is my lord's property. I take care of."

He stepped closer, towering over her, and for a moment Cynara thought the bluff had failed. Her hand slid toward her boot, fingers brushing the hilt of her vinte. Maltron, watching from the shadows, tensed to intervene.

Then Linhok's growl rolled out from the cargo crates—low, dangerous, unmistakable. The alien froze, eyes darting toward the sound. Cynara seized the moment, jamming the loader into gear. The machine jolted forward, nearly clipping the alien's leg. He stumbled back, muttering a curse, but didn't press further.

Cynara exhaled slowly, sweat prickling her brow. The bluff had held, but barely. She guided the loader toward the shuttle, the warning light still flickering on the panel. Damon hurried alongside, checking the fuel line connection. "It's not stable," he hissed. "If we don't fix this, the engines will choke."

"Then fix it," Cynara snapped, eyes locked on the shuttle ramp.

Bethayne and Travis slipped inside, pretending to check pressurization controls. Travis shot her a quick signal—two fingers raised, then a fist. *Not ready yet.*

Cynara clenched her jaw. Every second they lingered risked discovery. The alien she'd bluffed was still watching from the edge of the deck, muttering to another worker. She could feel the tension tightening around them like a net.

"Move faster," she whispered to Maltron, her voice sharp. "We don't get a second chance."

FLOODLIGHTS CARVED HARD SHADOWS beneath the shuttle's belly, the ground crew moving like clockwork between hoses and consoles. Maltron kept his head down and his eyes busy, counting bodies, gauging angles, memorizing rhythms. The vessel's curved hull, sleek and alien, wore Heliotian markings that caught and swallowed the light. He didn't like unknowns, but tonight they didn't have anything else.

"Doesn't look like anything from Ama City's fleet," he murmured.

Cynara didn't look up. "I can get it moving," she said quietly. "Landing… we'll worry about later."

Maltron grunted. Worry could wait. Motion came first.

Travis slid nearer, peering at a diagnostic panel through the open maintenance hatch. "Pressurization shows green, but the system flags an override pending," he whispered. "If they launch with that, someone will have to confirm it from the bay."

Bethayne stood a little too straight behind him, trying to look invisible and confident at the same time. Maltron angled his body to block her from the technician's casual sweep of attention. "We'll confirm it," he said. "Fast."

Cynara moved, a worker's stride and a worker's focus, head tipped, shoulders square. Maltron saw the torn sleeve before anyone else did—ragged edge, wired shut, the dark stain she couldn't scrub out. He felt his stomach tighten. It could pass as old, it could pass as careless. It could also draw the wrong eye.

She reached for the pressurization console and faltered, just a breath—her injured hand stiffening as she caught the edge and shifted her weight. The movement was small, quick; the jaw set was not. She punched the override through, and the gauge rolled from amber to green.

A technician turned, squinting at her sleeve. Maltron's shoulder dipped, his stance ready, but Cynara spoke first, voice pitched low and rough.

"Caught it on a piece of equipment," she said, tugging the torn edge as if to hide it. "My blood. Nothing serious."

The man frowned, undecided. Then the fuel pressure alarm chirped from the far station, and he swiveled back to his post. Maltron let out a slow breath.

"Time to move," Cynara whispered.

They flowed with the workers toward the ramp. Linhok vanished beneath a parked dolly, then reappeared along the shadow line of the cargo supports and slipped up into the bay. Travis and Bethayne peeled off into the passenger access, heads down, hands busy, every motion borrowed from someone who belonged. Cynara stepped onto the ramp and Maltron close behind her, holding a cable coil like he meant it.

Inside, the shuttle felt tighter than Araman builds—narrower aisle, lower overhead, controls arranged like the Heliotians thought differently in every way. Maltron took it all in without stopping. He crossed to the cargo bay bulkhead door and checked the latch; sealed, but the manual release was accessible. Good.

Cynara dropped to one knee by the fuel intake and pulled the side panel. The fittings were familiar enough, but the warning indicator pulsed in an odd rhythm. "Not stable," Maltron muttered, crouching with her. "They've got a backflow dampener that's keyed different."

"Can you anchor it?" she asked.

He slid his fingers in, feeling the flex give—one notch, then another. "If the dampener trips at launch, we choke."

Cynara braced the line with her good hand, the injured one trembling as she steadied the connection. "Do it," she said. Her tone was sharp, but he knew where the edge came from.

Together they forced the line home. The indicator flickered—amber, amber, green—and stayed. Maltron tested the feed twice, then let out the breath he'd been holding. "It'll hold."

Footsteps sounded at the ramp. Cynara stood quickly, pulling the panel shut. Maltron moved to the side console and put his hand on a lever, blocking the view of the wiring Cynara had pinned earlier. Two Heliotian crewmen paused at the threshold, exchanging quick words in their own tongue. The taller one looked past them at the cargo stacks. Maltron shifted his stance again—still, ordinary, just another worker on a routine night.

The men stepped inside and continued forward toward the cockpit. Maltron didn't move until their voices faded. Then he turned to Cynara. "Crew of three?"

She nodded once. "Pilot, copilot, loadmaster."

"Bethayne and Travis?"

"In the passenger aisle," she said. "If anyone questions them, they're checking seat restraints."

Maltron crossed to the cargo bay door and cracked the manual lever. Pressurized air hissed behind the seam; intact and sealed. The bay beyond was stacked with nets and crates, the kind of place a person could disappear if they knew where to look. Linhok's eyes flashed from beneath a slung tarp. The cat's tail flicked and stilled.

"Before launch, we stow," Maltron said. Cynara's gaze met his and held. For the first time since he'd watched her pull a torn, bloodied sleeve over an injured hand and bluff a stranger, he let the admiration show. Not in words—he didn't have time for those—but in the way he nodded and turned to make space for her.

They worked fast. Maltron checked the cargo net anchors, tugged each tie, picked a line of bundles that wouldn't shift under acceleration. Cynara climbed the support struts, breath tight, trying not to use the injured hand and having to anyway. She slipped, catching herself with a hiss. Maltron reached up, stabilizing her boot with a palm. She nodded a thank-you without looking down, then wrapped her wrists into the net and settled as though she'd done it a hundred times.

"Travis," Maltron called softly toward the aisle. "Find your brace."

"I've got Bethayne," Travis whispered back from the shadows. "We're strapped at the rear seats."

The loadmaster's voice carried from the cockpit. Maltron couldn't parse the words, but the cadence sounded like checklists. He ducked into the passenger compartment long enough to see the stretchers and seats—one injured alien at the back, strapped down. The man's face was slack. Maltron counted heads again—six passengers, three crew. Eleven to clear if it came to that. Ten if the unconscious one stayed out. Those odds still looked better than the numbers they'd faced in the Ama City streets.

He slipped back into the bay and pulled the door shut behind him. Floodlights washed the seams for a beat, then dimmed. Outside, ground crew shouted, a whistle blew, and the ramp began to retract.

Cynara shifted in the net, jaw tight. Maltron took his place opposite her, wedging his shoulders against bundled cargo and hooking his arms through the mesh. The torn sleeve of her disguise brushed the rope, and he saw her mouth flatten at the scrape—small pain, big launch ahead. She breathed out once, in control.

The ship shuddered. A hum built under their feet—deeper than Araman engines, with a higher vibration threading it. Maltron adjusted his brace. The dampener indicator he'd watched earlier blinked once on the bay panel and went dark again. Good.

A klaxon sounded from the forward section; the copilot's voice answered in short bursts. The shuttle eased forward, turned, and the walls around them thrummed with the alignment. Then the engines fired, slamming weight down and back. The cargo shifted a hand's width—nets caught, anchors held. Maltron grit his teeth and pressed into the motion, riding the pull until it steadied.

Cynara closed her eyes and tightened her grip until her knuckles whitened. She didn't speak. She didn't need to. He could see every note of what she was fighting in the set of her shoulders and the way she refused to let the tremor travel past her wrist.

They climbed. Arama's gravity clawed at the hull, then loosened, then tried again. Maltron felt the dampener pulse once beneath them as fuel flow rebalanced; it held. He breathed out slowly through his nose, measuring the seconds. Somewhere in the passenger compartment, a restraint ratcheted. In the cockpit, a checklist switched from ascent to glide.

The hum softened as the shuttle reached steady climb. The pounding in Maltron's arms receded to a hard throb. He glanced across at Cynara. She opened her eyes, met his look, and the two of them counted a beat together.

"Half an hour once we're off the ground," she'd said. He held that number now like a plan and a promise.

He scanned the bay again, mapping what came next. The manual to the main cabin sat mid-wall to his left; once they were clear of Arama's gravity well, they'd need to move through it fast—seal the control pod, break the crew's rhythm, and keep the passengers pinned long enough to lock down. Travis and Bethayne would need a signal. Linhok would need a lane.

Maltron shifted his weight, testing the net. It would hold until they were ready. He let his breath ease in and out, syncing to the shuttle's vibration, and told himself the same thing he told his men when a fight hung in the balance: break it into steps, and take the first one clean.

Across from him, Cynara loosened her grip a fraction, the flicker of pain passing, the resolve staying. Torn sleeve, injured hand, and an awkward lie that had worked because she wore it with straight-backed nerve. He wondered how many times tonight he would owe survival to that quiet, stubborn will.

The shuttle leveled, engines settling into their long climb. Maltron closed his eyes for a heartbeat and pictured the next door opening, the next corridor, the next choice. Then he opened them, checked the anchors one more time, and held on. The gravity would let go soon. When it did, they'd move.

Chapter Twenty-Three

Crossing Thresholds

THE SHUTTLE ROLLED OUT across the field and then tilted up at an eighty-five-degree angle just before the engines fired to launch her toward Arama's moon. Beyond that celestial body, still well out of detection range, Y'riel's warship—a balloon of metal large enough to swallow dozens of Minoan shuttles—awaited her return.

"A beautiful sight," Y'riel breathed as she watched the launch with increasing satisfaction. The first riches her troops had plundered in Ama City were on the way to her ship. More than that, grains, wheat, and rice also rose on the shuttle. Food for her people, she thought. Enough food to begin easing the hunger in her world. That provided the main motivation for coming to this solar system.

The Heliotian system was not as blessed as this one. The children of Astara, as the natives called their life star, lived on fair worlds by comparison. Within this single star system, three habitable planets supported natural life with abundant vegetation. Four, if one counted the satellite they called Corlan. Even on planets not truly habitable, the people of this system lived and survived.

But Helios did not have the likes of this. Her own planet, Hitara, baked under the hot star and grew drier every year. In a few small pockets, they'd established hydroponic farms where they grew food with minimal water. And in the caves to the north, they could produce a few other edibles, but not enough. Not anymore.

Once there had been abundant food, water, and habitable land, but time changed all that. The population increased, the sun grew hotter, and available water receded. If she expected to maintain her control of Helios, this takeover of the Astara system needed to succeed. The people demanded food and riches, and the one who ruled must provide them.

She turned away from the spaceport window, glimpsed one of her soldiers hovering near, and folded her arm back at the elbow with fist clenched—a sign of success. The soldier acknowledged with a flicker of a smile, then resumed guard of his Empress.

"Come, Y'Tauk," she said to the officer waiting by the door. "We have much to do and this fabled sorceress to locate. We will soon issue a statement to all cities that their capital has fallen and we have gained control. We'll advise them their protectors have failed, and they should prepare to surrender as we come to their municipality. I don't foresee much more fighting to conquer the planet, although we might encounter pockets of resistance." Y'riel began walking toward the exit.

"What about the natives of this planet?" Y'Tauk asked as he fell into step beside her. "What do we do with them?"

"They're farmers," she said with an unpleasant smile. "They shall farm for as long as they live. Of course, we shall have to control them and keep the numbers down, but they should be adequate for our needs." She paused to glance at him. "Your task is to locate Princess Cynara, the so-called sorceress. Find her and her companions, apprehend them, and bring them to me. I will make an example of her."

TRAVIS AND BETHAYNE CLUNG to each other as the shuttle gained height. He had slid painfully into the corner of the maintenance locker where they'd hidden themselves, and Bethayne crashed into him as soon as the shuttle lifted her nose. At first, they interlocked arms and legs like a piece of ancient interlacing artwork. Still, amid many pokes and shoves, they sorted themselves out. Travis urged the girl in front of him and wrapped his arms around her waist to hold her.

"That was frightening," she whispered. She still trembled from the near-vertical liftoff.

Travis confessed silently to being somewhat frightened himself. He'd read about shuttle launches and imagined what one would be like dozens of times. However, reality exceeded his fantasies, especially without the luxury of an actual seat.

Briefly, he wondered how the Princess and her two companions had fared on liftoff and how they would manage to rendezvous at the right time. For now, his main concern was not getting crushed under Bethayne's weight as they continued climbing.

The force proved incredible, pressure bearing down harder than he'd ever imagined. Just when he felt his rib cage might cave in, the heavy thrust ceased, and the pressure lightened.

"Second stage," Travis murmured.

Bethayne breathed heavily, eyes still squeezed shut. "What does that mean?"

He eased her gently forward. "It means the main thrust is over. We've pierced through the gravitational field. That required the most power. Now we only need booster thrust to push the shuttle to her destination."

She opened her eyes and twisted to look at him. "I don't understand. What's a gravitational field?"

"It's what allows us to walk and move around on the planet's surface. If it weren't for this shuttle's artificial gravity, we'd be floating now." Travis eased himself to his feet and stretched his taut muscles. "This is quite a ship—beautifully designed. The fuel tanks hold more than enough to get us to Corlan. In fact, they probably hold enough to get us to Minos."

"This is all pretty complex to me, Travis. I know plants and healing, but this—" She gestured around them. "—this is totally out of my world. It's the most frightening thing I've ever gone through." Her voice broke with nervous tension.

Travis bent down to pull her to her feet, then steadied her in his arms. "The worst of it is over now. From here on, it should be a gentle ride. Of course, we still must take over the ship." Unconsciously, he stroked her hair while she wrapped her arms around him and clung tightly. Travis looked down into her small, delicate face, seeing trust in her eyes.

Feelings of strength and confidence flowed through him. He wanted to protect this girl and take care of her. It didn't resemble the feelings he'd had with Dawnha, nor the compelling desire to protect the Princess. For a moment, he felt a pang of guilt as he recalled his commitment to Cynara. Still, after defeating this invasion, nothing stood in the way of being with Bethayne.

The Princess was not for him; he'd known that from the moment he met her. Even though they were close in age, her whole demeanor spoke of ancient power.

Slowly, with only slight hesitation, his face moved closer to Bethayne's. She tilted her head higher to meet his until their lips almost touched.

Abruptly, the door to the compartment slid aside. Travis jerked away from Bethayne and fumbled for the weapon at his waist.

"It's a good thing we're not enemies," Cynara said softly. "Come quickly before someone enters this corridor."

Travis grabbed Bethayne's hand and pulled her out behind him. Cynara was already moving along the corridor, her footsteps silent on the carpeted walkway. Travis glanced in the opposite direction, heart thudding as he checked for movement, then started after her. Where she walked along the side, the ceiling almost touched her head, but toward the middle it curved four inches higher. She glanced back and motioned sharply for them to hurry, then slipped around a corner to the right.

As Travis rounded it, he found another partially open door. Cautiously, he stepped through and emerged into a locker room with two racks of pressure suits—and the frost leopard. Once Bethayne was through, he punched the button to close the door the rest of the way and studied the area. He spotted an airlock at the end of the room and a crawlway off to the right.

Linhok blinked at them, yawned, then started through the crawlway.

"I guess we'd better follow," Travis whispered, dropping to hands and knees and going after the cat.

The crawlway surface was smooth metal and reasonably level. In two places, he had to push himself with his toes to get up the slight rises. He marveled that Linhok managed them at all. Bethayne, keeping up with apparent ease, stayed close behind him. At one point, he thought he heard voices—but then it went quiet again, leaving him unsure..

Eventually, they reached a break in the crawlway that led right again, sloped down slightly, and exited into a noisy room. The sound of the ship's engines was intense here, vibrating through the floor. Large gray metallic-looking boxes were bolted to the deck, and the sharp smell of electrical wiring filled the air. A slight breeze from the cooling system brushed his hair as he crawled out. Twisting, he helped Bethayne down, then looked around.

Cynara was only a few feet away, beaming with a cheerful grin. "United again." She nodded toward one of the metal boxes, and Travis followed her motion. Maltron peered intently at an indicator panel.

"The ship's memory banks?" Travis guessed, pressing his hand against the nearest box with a sense of reverence.

"Right," Cynara answered. "The main control center of the shuttle. They have terminals on the control pod, but this is the core. The thruster engines are on the other side of that wall. How much do you know about the shuttle?"

"Not enough. There's only so much the learning tapes show you, and this one isn't like ours." He stepped toward the bank of indicators Maltron was studying. "Are we looking for something in particular?"

"I think I found it," Maltron replied, excitement sharpening his voice. "I just need to be certain which area to shut down."

"What are you trying to shut down?"

"The oxygen supply to the passenger cabin."

"You're not going to suffocate those people?" Bethayne asked sharply.

"No, of course not. Even if I wanted to, the ship would eventually override the manual shutdown and begin supplying enough oxygen to keep them alive. I just want them to pass out so we don't have to deal with them. If I could do the same thing in the pod, I would."

Edging next to Maltron, Travis studied the indicators and controls. He didn't think he'd ever seen so many colored lights and gauges. If they were like Minoan ones, they monitored the ship's functions—surface temperature, speed, heading, and other operations. You could control the shuttle from down here if you knew how. The ones Maltron focused on were labeled with an odd symbol Travis couldn't read and were arranged in a row of four amber lights. Beneath each was a flat square switch shoved into the up position.

"You select the wrong one, and you could cut off our air," Travis warned.

"That's a possibility," Maltron agreed. "Got any ideas?"

"How do you know we won't set off an alarm if we hit any of the buttons?"

"We don't," Cynara responded. "But it's our best option, Travis. Even if we set off an alarm and one or two crewmen come to check it out, we have the odds in our favor."

He nodded, studying the lights and thinking through the shuttle's structure. The engineers had likely lined the switches up in the same order as the ship's compartments. He glanced left—toward the shuttle's nose. Next would be the cargo bay and crew lounge, then the passenger compartment, and finally the aft cargo bay and engines.

"The third one," he said finally. "That should be the passenger compartment."

"I agree. The symbols resemble an unspoken language, similar to the way I communicate with Linhok." Cynara gave a single nod. Maltron pressed the switch.

For a few heartbeats, nothing happened. No change in sound, no change in the indicator. Then the amber light winked out, replaced by a red beam blinking intermittently.

Cynara's eyes met Maltron's. "The same signal will be flashing on the bridge."

"And someone will be down here to check it out," Travis added.

Although no one spoke, a silent command seemed to pass between them as each found a place out of sight.

Travis deposited Bethayne in a safe place between two memory modules, then found a spot for himself near the controls. Tucked behind another module for cover, he could watch the opening they'd come through. Any kind of energy weapon used in this room could be disastrous. He worried the others didn't realize it—until he glimpsed Maltron crouched nearby, weapon still at his waist.

Linhok hovered just out of sight near the crawlway opening. The substantial white cat crouched low, ready to spring. His ears flicked forward, listening.

Travis spotted Cynara stationed on the other side of the room next to another crawlway door—this one still shut. While they expected investigators from the front of the ship, they couldn't ignore the aft section. Travis watched her slide the vinte from her boot into her hand. She stood poised for attack.

During the wait, it seemed no one even breathed. *Maybe the crew can override the command*, Travis thought anxiously. But a quick glance at the console showed the red light still blinking.

He detected a subtle movement from Linhok as his muscles rippled in anticipation.

A scraping sound followed. An alien soldier pulled himself through the vent shaft, rising to his feet. He froze as his eyes locked on Linhok crouched a yard away.

Travis wondered why the cat hadn't already attacked when a metallic blur sliced through the air and drove straight into the Heliotian's chest. The soldier's face registered shock, his hand reaching for the embedded weapon before he pitched forward.

As Travis watched, the vinte dislodged itself from the victim and floated back into Cynara's waiting hand. He drew in a deep breath and resumed watching the crawlspace opening. Clearly, the princess expected more.

Chapter Twenty-Four

Don't Damage Anything Vital

DAMON MALTRON REMAINED ALERT as he flattened himself against a control box. While his weapon stayed holstered, his hand rested on the battle taser in his pocket. Small though it was, he knew it could deliver a heavy jolt if he got close enough to use it.

The princess stepped back into shadow, palm extended in a silent command to wait. Maltron held still, counting the minutes until she moved forward again. "We'll have to go after the rest of them," she said.

Maltron nodded. "The ship's automatic system will override that command pretty soon. I doubt they'll send anyone else."

Cynara wiped her vinte clean on the fallen Heliotian's uniform and slipped into the access vent following Linhok. Maltron crawled forward, guessing Bethayne would be next, with Travis at the rear.

Caution was second nature to him. Being a mercenary had taught him that much. He slid his laser weapon into his hand as he reached the branch in the crawlway—and the precaution saved his life.

Another Heliotian appeared head-on. Both men fired almost simultaneously. Maltron dropped flat, feeling the heat of the laser ruffle his hair as it scorched past. He brought his head up, fired again, and saw his shot strike true. The alien sprawled lifeless in the tube. Maltron exhaled, relief sharp in his chest.

A touch on his arm made him tense, but Cynara's whisper steadied him. "Are you all right?"

"Just singed a little. I hope there are no more. I might not be so lucky next time. This is not the ideal location to meet someone."

"We'll have to shove him out as we go or try to crawl over him," she said.

Maltron grimaced. "I'm the largest of us; let's see if I can get over him."

Distastefully, he slid across the alien's body, elbows digging, shoulders straining. The corpse shifted easily on the slick metal, dragging along with him. Cynara grabbed the ankles and pulled back as Maltron forced his way past. At last, his shoulders cleared, and he pulled himself forward.

Breathing hard, he motioned her back. "Better idea. You slide into the side crawlway, and I'll shove him straight through to the opposite junction."

"Good thinking," she agreed. She stepped back, motioned to Linhok, and told Bethayne to slide back so they could get in front of her.

Once they'd repositioned themselves, Maltron braced his feet against the dead man's shoulders and shoved. The body slid forward, momentum carrying it deeper into the branch. He repeated the action twice more until the corpse had shifted nearly two meters into the other arm. Then he flipped onto his knees and resumed crawling. Cynara followed, the others trailing behind.

A commotion stirred behind him—Bethayne's voice, sharp with curiosity: "What are you doing?" Maltron didn't hear the answer. Whatever it was, they'd sort it out once clear of the tunnel.

He emerged into the locker, straightened, and offered a hand to Cynara. She hopped down without help. He steadied Bethayne next, then waited for Travis. The boy wasn't immediately behind.

"Where's Travis?" Maltron asked.

"He turned the opposite way at the junction," Bethayne said, frowning. "I don't know why. He didn't answer me."

Maltron shrugged, annoyance prickling. He started back into the crawlway but stopped when Travis appeared, crawling toward him. Maltron stepped aside, waiting as the teenager dropped down.

"What kept you?" Cynara demanded.

Travis grinned, pulling two objects from his clothing. "These." He held up a laser weapon and a communication device. "I figured the alien didn't need them anymore."

Maltron chuckled. "Good thinking, farm boy."

He closed the vent and motioned them forward. "Take a deep breath and get through the passenger cabin quickly. The shuttle override provides enough oxygen to sustain life but not consciousness. At least, I hope no one's come around yet."

He opened the door, scanning the nodding heads—six passengers, all unconscious. That meant the two who had investigated earlier were from this group, leaving three crew in the control pod. Maltron hurried through, motioning the others to follow.

Cynara stopped to pat down a passenger, pulling a weapon from his clothing. Travis did the same, adding another to his growing stash. Maltron urged them on. Bethayne and Linhok reached his side, breath held, waiting. The others joined them armed, each carrying at least one weapon stripped from the passengers.

Maltron shoved the crew door open, inhaling fresh air as he did.

"IT SEEMS NO WELL-DRESSED HELIOTIAN is without a personal weapon," Cynara said dryly as Maltron closed the door behind them. "Tells you a lot about their society. Can we seal this cabin off in case they wake up?"

Maltron studied the controls, shaking his head. "Not unless we break them completely, and I'm not sure even that would work."

"Try it," Cynara ordered.

While Maltron worked on the door, she inspected the crew lounge—a small cabin with bunks, a cooker, beverage dispenser, and lavatory. Functional, but nothing more. Her eyes stayed fixed on the connecting door to the control pod. This next step would be the most dangerous.

"Door's jammed," Maltron said softly, joining her. "That's only this side, though. There should be three of them up front."

She nodded. "You, me, and Linhok."

He grinned. "That's the way I see it. We'll have to be careful not to damage anything vital."

Cynara relayed silent instructions to Linhok. The cat moved up alongside her, muscles coiled.

Travis slipped closer. "What do you want Bethayne and me to do?"

"Guard this room and be our backup. If anything happens to me, take out whoever's left in the pod and fly the shuttle to Corlan. If you get through, tell them the Princess flies without their guidance. They'll know what it means." She motioned him back and nodded to Maltron.

The door slid open with a hiss of air. Cynara dropped low, somersaulting into the cabin behind the pilot's chair. Linhok followed, a white blur that landed in the navigator's lap. Maltron went in last, low and weapon ready, aiming for the co-pilot.

Even with surprise on their side, they still had a battle ahead.

THE FROST LEOPARD LUNGED for the navigator, but the man twisted, blocking his throat. Linhok tore at the alien's arms instead, claws raking flesh, blood slicking the controls. The navigator fought to bring his laser around, grip stubborn even as his hands shredded.

Linhok pressed harder, body slamming into the man's arms until his jaws locked on the throat. The alien thrashed, squeezed off one wild shot that singed fur and exploded against the upper interface, then went limp beneath the leopard's crushing hold.

CYNARA'S QUARRY MOVED FOR his weapon the instant the door opened. He was already half out of his chair when she completed her roll. The barrel swung toward her, but she lashed out, her leg catching his knee and throwing him off balance. His shot went wide.

She pounced, mimicking her companion's feral strike, vinte flashing in her hand. The Heliotian swung the butt of his weapon, grazing her head. Pain jolted, but she pressed forward, driving the blade into his chest and up. His scream tore through the cabin before his body crashed to the floor, twitching until it stilled.

The co-pilot reacted slower, but his weapon was already out, aimed at Linhok. Cynara glimpsed Maltron's low pivot, his hand driving the taser into the alien's side. His hand jerked involuntarily firing his weapon, scorching controls above his head. Maltron's return fire struck true. The co-pilot pitched forward, and the shuttle rocked violently before leveling again.

Cynara braced herself against the pilot's chair, exhaustion creeping into her limbs. Her hand throbbed, and she rubbed it instinctively, but her grin broke through the fatigue. She thrust her arm upward in victory.

Maltron straightened, scanning the carnage. The frost leopard peered over the navigator's seat, white fur splattered with blood. Cynara met his gaze, breath ragged.

"I think we've done it," Maltron laughed. "Is everyone okay? Is the cat okay?"

"Yes," Cynara gasped. "He's fine. All we have to do now is determine how much damage was done—and figure out how to fly this thing."

Chapter Twenty-Five

Does This Thing Fly Automatically?

TRAVIS SWEPT HIS GAZE across the control pod, taking in the scorched panels and flickering indicators, and muttered, "I told you not to hit anything vital."

Maltron shrugged. "Their weapons were aimed the wrong direction. But the lower control decks are sound."

Travis leaned over the console, eyes darting across the alien symbols. Some resembled diagrams he'd seen in training tapes, but others were jagged glyphs that meant nothing to him. He muttered under his breath, trying to match shapes to functions.

The console gave off a faint warmth, and a soft crackle from somewhere beneath hinted at stressed wiring.

The shuttle hummed steadily, locked on its pre-set course. "It's running on autopilot," he said. "If we want to change direction, we'll have to talk to the computer."

Cynara stood beside him, pale, her injured hand pressed against the pilot's chair. She gave a short nod. "On our ships, there was never any need for passwords. Whoever sat here had the right to command. Maybe they're the same."

When he glanced her way, he saw Bethayne wiping blood from the deck, her movements quick and nervous. The faint scrape of cloth on metal carried through the tense quiet. Maltron had already dragged the bodies into the lounge. Linhok crouched nearby, ears flicking at every sound.

Travis keyed in the coordinates Cynara dictated. The console blinked, but then a screen with a reply box showed. "Password or code," he muttered.

With a frown, Cynara knelt by the dead pilot and searched for anything that might have the password on it. She found a scannable ID card and handed it to Travis. "Try this."

Taking the metallic-feeling card, he held it to the screen. A brief scan line read it and the box disappeared. Travis entered the coordinates again. The console blinked twice, and the shuttle gradually shifted into a shallow arc away from Y'reil's warship.

Relief loosened the tightness in his chest. "We're clear—for now."

But the alien symbols kept flashing. Travis frowned, tracing one that looked like a stabilizer control. "This one… I think it's for balance." He pressed it.

The shuttle lurched violently, nose dipping. Alarms shrieked. The deck pitched under his boots, throwing his stomach into his throat. Bethayne cried out, clutching the chair. Cynara staggered, her injured hand slamming against the console and she cursed.

"Travis!" Maltron barked.

Travis's heart pounded. He slammed another glyph, guessing function from its placement. The shuttle steadied, alarms cutting off. He exhaled hard, sweat beading on his forehead. His hands trembled slightly on the controls. "Okay—okay. That was trim control. Got it now."

Cynara's voice was sharp but steady. "No more guesses."

Travis nodded, jaw tight. "I can fly this. I just need to read the logic. Symbols are grouped navigation, thrust, stabilizers. It's like a puzzle."

Maltron muttered, "Puzzle or death trap."

Abruptly, the comms crackled. A burst of static made Travis flinch before the harsh alien voice cut through. The message repeated, sharper each time.

Bethayne whispered, "They've noticed."

Cynara spun to the navigation console, activating a secondary screen. "That's a scanner. Damon, keep watch. If anything shows up, warn us."

Travis's hands hovered over the controls, pulse racing. "If this thing doesn't fly itself, we'll have to take it to manual. And I think I can."

Cynara pressed her injured hand against the chair, pain etched across her face. "Then it's yours, Travis. Get us to Corlan."

ON BOARD THE HELIOTIAN mother ship, the communications officer turned to his commander, Y'haleran, and reported the lack of response. The small, dark-haired woman, who bore a striking resemblance to her sister Y'riel, frowned, worry clouding her black eyes.

There was no time to contact the Empress for instructions, and Y'haleran hated making decisions. But one must be made now. Drawing a long, slow breath, she said, "Radio again for instant explanations. Inform them we will be forced to launch pursuit ships unless they resume the course to us."

The officer nodded and repeated her message to the shuttle. Y'haleran waited, hoping she was doing what her sister would do. When it became evident they would get no response, she ordered the pursuit ships launched. Most certainly, she told herself, this was the correct action, and even the Empress would do the same.

In that, she was right—except the Empress would not have hesitated. Y'haleran's hesitation cost her dearly.

"ISN'T THERE ANY WAY to get this thing to move faster?" Damon asked anxiously.

The two blips on his screen were closing fast. They'd appeared on the edge of the scanner barely twenty minutes earlier and were moving faster than anything Travis had ever seen on a scanner.

"We're at maximum speed now," the Princess answered. "This ship wasn't designed for speed or for battle. We're not far from Corlan, and I think we'll still make it ahead of them."

She pressed an indicator on the scanner to shift to forward view. The outline of Corlan appeared, swelling larger as they drew nearer. Travis heard the hitch in Cynara's breath as half a ring marked by dots sprang up around the small planet.

"The defense shield is activated."

"What?" Damon demanded.

UNKNOWN SHUTTLE. IDENTIFY IMMEDIATELY.

The booming voice from Corlan startled everyone except Cynara, who had expected it. It vibrated through the deck plates, a low resonance Travis felt in his ribs.

She activated the communications console. “This is Princess Cynara in control of the shuttle. We are coming in with no shuttle crew and two Heliotian ships in pursuit. We’ll need guidance and Controllers.”

ACKNOWLEDGED. KEY IN YOUR IDENTITY CODE, PRINCESS.

Swiftly, she punched the code into the computer and waited impatiently while it was transmitted. Her fingers tapped a rapid rhythm on the console, the soft clicks sharp in the tense silence.

STAY ON YOUR COURSE. WE WILL MAKE A POCKET IN THE SCREEN BASED ON YOUR CURRENT COURSE. CONTROLLERS WILL BE READY ONCE YOU HAVE ENTERED THE ATMOSPHERE.

“Thanks to Tiel,” she murmured, switching the scanner back to rear view. The sight was grim: one of the pursuit ships was now dangerously close. Travis felt a cold knot form in his stomach. “I think we’re in for trouble.”

“I don’t suppose there are any weapons on this ship,” Damon asked dryly. “Those ships will be within attack range in seconds.”

“I told you it wasn’t built for battle.”

"So, what do we do?" Travis asked. "It looks clear ahead, but I don't see an opening in the field yet."

The engines whined, protesting the increased speed.

"We hang on and pray to Tiel we reach that screen before those ships can destroy us." Cynara laid her hand on Damon's shoulder, leaning toward the scanner to watch the advancing ships.

Travis reached for Bethayne's hand and urged her into the co-pilot's chair. "Better prepare for a rough trip," he said, giving her an encouraging smile.

At maximum output, the engines strained, the vibration running up through the deck and into Travis's boots.

A SMALL BLIP PULSED ON the scanner — close, too close.

"They're firing," Maltron said, his voice dead calm.

"Everyone, hang on," Cynara ordered. She turned, spotting Linhok wedged into a shallow well between the door and the central computer bank. Maltron's arm looped around her waist, pulling her down.

"We're short a seat," he explained. "You can't just stand there."

The sudden pull stole her breath — his arm firm across her stomach, his chest solid behind her. For a heartbeat her body went rigid, instinct and something sharper flaring before she shoved the reaction aside. Survival first. Everything else later.

Travis jerked the shuttle into an evasive maneuver that would have knocked her off her feet if she hadn't been seated. The hull groaned under the sudden strain, a loose panel overhead rattling like teeth in a jar. The first torpedo streaked past beneath them — she caught the flash of it on the scanner — and the second ship launched another.

Cynara closed her eyes, forcing her focus to the shuttle's rear. Maltron rubbed her arm as she went rigid with effort. She pictured a shield — a sheet of energy wrapping the vessel. She envisioned the torpedo approaching, two more behind it, and tried to strengthen the web.

The first torpedo struck the shield and exploded harmlessly. The boom reverberated through the cabin, a deep vibration that buzzed in her bones. The second followed, detonating before impact. But the third came too quickly. Her energy faltered, the shield broke, and the weapon slammed into the shuttle's left side.

Cynara gasped, jerking as the torpedo penetrated. The shuttle lurched violently, throwing her weight against Maltron. A sharp, acrid scent of overheated circuitry stung her nose as something behind the console sizzled. She gulped for air, eyes flying open — and saw a red warning light flashing across Travis's console.

"Our course is altered slightly," Travis said, scanning the screens. She saw the color drain from his face. "That one caught our right outward thruster."

"I couldn't stop it," Cynara admitted, breath ragged. "We've got to get the ship back on the exact course. Is the computer correcting?"

Travis shook his head. Cynara pushed herself out of Maltron's lap, leaning over the console. Another torpedo grazed the shuttle's edge, jolting her into Travis. A metallic clatter erupted behind them — something small breaking loose and skittering across the deck. He caught her before she slammed into the controls. She ignored the shuddering frame, fingers flying as she keyed in the original course.

The shuttle rolled sharply, and Cynara braced herself against the console as the motion tugged her sideways. The thrusters whined in protest, a high, strained pitch that made her teeth ache. She checked the readouts, frowned, and entered another correction. Again, the shuttle veered, aligning closer.

"Go to the forward scan," she shouted at Damon. "How close are we?"

"About fifteen seconds."

"Without that thruster, we won't be able to control it in the atmosphere," Travis warned.

Cynara made a third adjustment, jaw tight. "If we don't hit that shield right, we won't have to worry about it."

The course finally looked true. She launched herself back to the navigation console, eyes LOCKED on the scanner. There — the pocket in Corlan's defense shield, exactly where it needed to be. The shuttle angled toward it.

A dull thud echoed from the passenger cabin — one of the unconscious bodies rolling into the door as the shuttle pitched. Her stomach clenched at the entry angle, but there was no time for another correction.

"Hold on!" she cried, gripping Maltron's seat as the shuttle slipped through the opening.

Chapter Twenty-Six

THROUGH THE SHIELD

THE SHUTTLE SHUDDERED AS IF being shaken apart. Bethayne gasped and clung to her seat, her face a white mask of fear.

Unanchored, Cynara fell to her knees as Maltron's hands reached for her. The deck vibrated beneath her palms, a deep, bone-rattling tremor. For a horrible moment, her stomach lurched, her heart raced wildly. *Did I miss the pocket?* Each second stretched fivefold as the violent tremors continued. *It's never been like this. Are we going to burn up?*

She sensed Linhok's fear, but the leopard's thoughts were silent, accepting whatever fate befell them. Beneath it ran a calmness, absolute faith in her. That steadiness anchored her more than the deck beneath her knees.

Abruptly, the ship jerked hard to a downward angle, then steadied. A metallic groan rippled through the hull. Cynara glanced at the scanner; they were through the shield. Ahead, Corlan loomed, a purplish-blue sphere filling the view.

"We made it," she breathed.

Switching to rear scan, she saw the first Heliotian ship reach the shield. A blue flash sparked at the edge, and the vessel vanished.

The second pursuit ship altered course instantly, trying to follow. Too far behind, the pocket was closed. Moments later, that ship disintegrated as it touched the shield.

"OH, MERCIFUL GODS!" Y'HALERAN'S eyes bulged as she observed the destruction. Her crew searched frantically for survivors, but only debris littered the void.

Shattered fragments drifted past the viewport, catching the cold light of the command deck. Her heart jerked as she recognized the insignia on a twisted piece of metal.

On weak knees, she sank into her command chair. *I've lost him.* Y'mar, her beloved mate, had commanded the second pursuit ship.

Then, through the shock, a more frightening thought emerged. *My sister will not forgive this.*

"Try to reach the Empress," she instructed, forcing her voice steady. Her hands trembled despite her effort to still them. Already she began to frame the shaded truth she would tell Y'riel.

"WHAT HAPPENED TO THE SHIPS?" Maltron exclaimed. "They just disappeared."

"They disintegrated when they hit the shield," Cynara said, pulling herself to her feet. "We'll be entering Corlan's atmosphere in about a minute, and that will be another jolt." She rubbed her knees, then opened a channel. "This is Princess Cynara. Do you have Controllers ready? We have damage to the left thruster."

Silence stretched, and she feared they'd lost communication. The only sound was the low hum of the overworked engines. Then the cabin filled with a voice:

CONTROLLERS ARE STANDING BY. ADJUST YOUR SHUTTLE ANGLE TEN DEGREES PLANETWARD. LEAVE COMMUNICATIONS OPEN FOR ADDITIONAL INSTRUCTIONS.

Cynara turned, but Travis's fingers were already flying across the console. Damon watched the scanner, his eyes fixed on the descending numbers, and he caught Cynara's hand, pulling her close. "Better get ready."

She nodded, settled back on his lap, gripping the chair's arm. She felt Maltron's heartbeat hammering a staccato rhythm and tension coiled through his body. He showed no fear on his face, but his pulse betrayed him.

The shuttle pierced the atmosphere, shaking violently. A roar like tearing metal filled her ears. Pressure forced her back against Maltron, his arms tightening around her. In a heartbeat, the ship adapted to compression and leveled — for a moment.

Then it rolled right, tilting to forty-five degrees. Cynara's eyes widened, lips tightening. Travis's face was pale but calm. "The nonfunctional thruster," he explained. "Without it, the shuttle will shift suddenly." He hesitated. "And we'll never be able to land it."

Silence followed. Cynara's mind raced through scenarios. Heat prickled along her skin as the shuttle fought the atmosphere. At last, Corlan's voice returned:

CONTROLLERS ARE PRESENT, PRINCESS. INSTRUCTIONS COMING. MAINTAIN CURRENT COURSE.

"Travis, can you keep the shuttle steady? No matter what happens?"

He scanned the console, nodded. "Yes. I'm pretty sure I can."

She eased out of Maltron's grip. "Do the best you can. I won't be able to help you." She braced against the wall, slid down cross-legged, and closed her eyes. Breathing deeply, she opened her mind to the Controllers.

Instructions flashed into her thoughts. Her astral core slipped free, a familiar pull, like stepping out of her own skin, moving into the damaged thruster. Fuel was intact, but the control valves had taken the full force of the torpedo. Automatic feeds were dead.

Following the Controllers' guidance, she sent jolts of energy to open the fuel flow, forcing the valves to respond. One Controller remained linked, steadying her. Another accessed the shuttle's guidance system, bypassing the crippled computer.

The shuttle rolled back, leveling out.

PUZZLED, TRAVIS NOTED THE CHANGE in the status of the left thruster. It appeared to be online with fuel flowing into the thruster engine, but the red malfunction light still blinked. He turned to stare at Cynara, who sat unmoving at the back of the pod, eyes closed, arms completely limp. Was she doing it? As he turned back to face the console, he met Maltron's eyes, which seemed to ask the same question. Travis shrugged, then checked their course.

They waited tensely as the shuttle came nearer and nearer to the ground, then came in on a landing approach to the shuttle port. The hum of the thrusters deepened, vibrating through the deck beneath his boots. Damon chewed at his lower lip and finally spoke. "Do you have to do anything to stop this contraption, Travis?"

"I don't know. All the adjustments and landing activities are being made automatically—or by something else." He looked back at the Princess again. "Or by her."

Maltron swallowed hard. "I hope somebody's stopping it."

"Me, too," Travis replied. He cast his eyes toward Bethayne, concerned for her safety. She'd squeezed her eyes shut and gripped the arms until her knuckles turned white. Clearly, as nervous as he was.

Linhok sat perfectly still, tail curled neatly around his paws, the picture of calm. Travis hoped the cat was communicating with the entranced princess. He prayed she had a handle on this because he didn't have a clue now. He turned his attention to the approach as the shuttle neared the flat field ahead.

As the ground loomed, landing wheels dropped with a heavy clunk, and the shuttle dipped toward the surface, hovering over it like a giant bird and descending gently. A soft jolt ran through the cabin as the wheels touched down. It rolled across the field, slowing steadily until it halted outside a tall, dome-shaped building.

"I don't believe it," Maltron said, letting his breath out. He'd been holding it ever since the shuttle touched the ground.

Travis caught Bethayne's hand and grinned. Relieved, he shouted, "We're here! We're really here."

RELEASED FROM HER TASK, Cynara slumped forward. Linhok rose from his safe spot to go to her and licked gently at her face. Slowly, she brought her head up and reached a gentle hand to the cat to rub his head. Yes. Safe, Linhok.

"Are you all right?"

Wearily, she looked up at Maltron, who hovered above her, concern etched in the tight set of his mouth. Her own mouth felt dry, and she ran her tongue over her lips before finally managing to croak an affirmative. His hands caught hers, pulling gently to help her to her feet, then his arm went around her to support her.

She raised her head, stared out through the front ports of the pod, and saw the beautiful blue and purple world of her birth. She smiled and laid her hand on Travis's shoulder. "Welcome to Corlan, my friends."

"I didn't think we were going to make it," Bethayne admitted.

"Neither did I," the Princess agreed. "Let's get out of this shuttle. Oh, the gravity is less on Corlan than on Arama, so movement will be easier. Walk carefully. Also, the air is thinner, so you might feel a little light-headed. One more thing — you are among very few people to visit Corlan, and you may find it quite strange. What you see here, you'll be asked to never reveal to anyone else."

Maltron's brows drew together at that, but he didn't speak. Travis, intent on the controls, pressed the release for the shuttle's outside hatch while Maltron unlocked the pod's door. He stepped through first, checked the still-secured entrance to the passenger cabin, and motioned the others toward the hatch at the end of the crew lounge.

As they started toward it, Damon glanced through the port into the passenger cabin. "Looks like our guests are starting to wake. They're going to be in for quite a surprise," he muttered with a satisfied smirk.

Travis followed Cynara down the steps from the shuttle, practically bouncing with each light-gravity stride. His eyes swept the surrounding area, wide with wonder. "It's more beautiful than I've ever dreamed," he said on a low breath.

Cynara's subdued smile showed her pleasure in his enthusiasm. She could feel the moisture in the air, almost tasting its sweetness. Thick groves of trees and shrubs in shades from the lightest blue to the deepest purple surrounded the entire port.

"I see why it appears mottled bluish—" Travis cut off, shock interrupting him as two humanoid creatures approached them.

"What are those?" Maltron asked, peering over Travis's shoulder.

"Those," Cynara responded warmly, a smile spreading across her face, "are two of my people. They are Ataran and Kalrah, the Controllers who helped land the shuttle." She noted the stunned look frozen on Travis's face. "They are of the Clan of Cantra."

Ataran and Kalrah bowed their heads slightly as they approached. Cynara stepped forward, her exhaustion hidden behind a smile.

"Controllers," she greeted warmly. "Your guidance saved us. I thank you in the name of Corlan."

Kalrah's eyes flicked toward the shuttle, where the unconscious passengers stirred. "You bring more than companions. You bring proof of Arama's fall."

Cynara's smile faded. She turned to her friends, then back to the Controllers. "Ama City has been taken. The Heliotians will not stop there. Arama's people are enslaved, and the Empress will press her advantage until she consumes this system. We cannot wait."

Ataran inclined his head. "The Clan has long prepared for this day. You are not alone."

Maltron stepped closer, his voice low but firm. "Then let's talk about what comes next. If Arama is to be freed, we'll need more than courage."

Cynara lifted her chin, her voice steady despite the ache in her body. "We will rally Corlan. We will gather allies from Minos and beyond. Arama will not remain in chains. The Clan of Cantra has returned, and together we will rise."

Bethayne's hand tightened around Travis's, her eyes wide with awe. Travis looked from Cynara to the Controllers, his face alight with the realization that this was only the beginning.

Above them, the sky of Corlan shimmered with the faint glow of the defense shield. Cynara gazed at it, her heart heavy with the memory of Ama City's fall yet burning with resolve.

"Tonight, we survived," she said softly. "Tomorrow, we fight."

Travis whispered, loud enough that she heard. "Strangers will come twice … one bringing death, one bringing friendship."

He looked at Cynara, then at the Controllers. "Maybe this is what it meant."

Cynara didn't answer. The rest of the prophecy pressed heavy in her mind: … and when the strangers walk among us, the hidden voices will rise.

She gazed at Ataran and Kalrah, knowing the words had begun to unfold.

End of Book One

To Be Continued in
RISING MAGEISTRA: RECALIBRATION
Coming in Winter 2026

From the Author:

If you have enjoyed this book, please leave a review wherever you purchased it or send me a note at:

LillianWolfe.author@gmail.com.

For an author, reader comments, praise, and sometimes criticism are the most rewarding aspect of writing. Your feedback is deeply appreciated, and reviews help other readers to find my books.

Thank you for reading. Lily

MAGEISTRA RISING is coming in December 2026. Read a teaser from the book right after the Glossary.

Glossary

Arama & Local Geography

Ama City – the central governing city on Arama, the most Earth-like planet in the Astara system.

Glass Mountains – the primary domain of the Kyreagles.

Tark Lonan – a key city in the north east of the

Weilock Center - university town to the north of Ama City

Wendford - A small town in the fertile southlands of Arama. Travis's hometown.

Transportation

Astral travel – the ability to allow the soul to leave the body and travel to any destination the person want it to go. A unique talent on Astara.

Skimmer – a suspended air vehicle built on Minos that uses the natural magnetic properties of the planets to lift the smaller and lighter personal travel vehicles for overland use.

Skyhopper - An airborne public transport vehicle — similar to a mini-bus — used on Arama and other inhabited worlds in the Astara system.

Wagoner - A three-wheeled cart designed by Travis for hauling supplies and navigating rough terrain.

Creatures

Antelare - a rabbit-like animal native to Corlan.

Freparda - A native cat-like animal from Polara. Similar in appearance to a frost leopard but wilder and untamed.

Frost Leopard - A pure-white, lion-sized big cat from Polara capable of forming a telepathic bond with a human. Linhok is the only frost leopard known to have bonded with anyone.

Redorfan – the most harvested food fish on Arama. Frequently a metaphor for doomed.

Zelebras - A biologically engineered animal native to Minos, resembling a cross between a gazelle and a zebra. Designed specifically to survive Minos's harsh environment.

Language & Expressions

Mageistra/Mageust – a sorceress or sorcerer, an elevated guardian genetically engineered by Corlan. Although titled Prince or Princess, their power includes magical-seeming abilities. Not all guardians are advanced to this level.

Osang - the alcoholic version of the drink made from sunberries

Sunberry cooler or tea - an unfermented drink made from sunberries, served chilled or warmed,

Tiel – Deity of Light and Truth, the Astartan godhead

Traca - unit of money about $2 dollars

Gynzara - A city on Corlan. Expression: *"When in Gynzara…"* — equivalent to "when in Rome," meaning follow the local customs or adapt to the culture around you.

Kyreagle Culture & Language

Bracil - The home grounds or territory of a coalition of Kyreagles.

Clatch - A regiment or organized group of Kyreagles.

Diag - The leader of the Kyreagles.

Ecorin – A trance-like state a Kyreagle affects when reciting the oral prophecy and ancestral legends of the Kyreagles, passed down through generations.

Kyereagle - an eagle-looking almost human-sized bird, very intelligent, and able to converse. Their faces bear almost human-looking features, somewhat like a harpy.

Kyeria - A single Kyreagle individual.

Mijia / Mijio - Kyreagle greetings. Mijia — used when addressing a female. Mijio — used when addressing a male.

Souuifan - the Kyreagle sacred record of history and prophecy.

Heliotian Empire Terms & Slang

Crum - A Heliotian derogatory term for a non-Heliotian.

h'yni - Heliotian measure of time referring to Hatara's rotation around its core sun.

Ha-shar taraq – the Heliotian equivalent to a ground skimmer vehicle that rides above the ground on an elevated stream of air.

Hatara - One of the Heliotian Empire's two inhabited worlds in the Helios system.

Hel-talek -Heliotian phrase meaning "my empress."

Hiverot - A term referring to the inhabitants of the cramped, clustered living quarters typical of the Heliotian race.

m'arks – A Heliotian unit of distance equal to roughly 500 meters (about 1,640 feet).

su-biz - Heliotian term meaning "ship's length."

Tools & Technology

Scanlite - A multi-purpose handheld instrument used to illuminate and scan non-organic items.

Skyhopper - An airborne public transport vehicle used on Arama and other inhabited worlds in the Astara system.

Wagoner - A three-wheeled cart designed by Travis for hauling supplies.

Astaran System Worlds

Corlan - a moon-sized inhabited world visible in Arama's sky. Originally settled by the first inhabitants of Arama, who later relocated there after new settlers arrived on Arama.

Astara – named after the governing star, the Earth-like planet is the heart of the system, the one ideally suited for agriculture, where the majority of the food for the system is raised. This is Cynara's assigned planet to protect, making her the key guardian of the system.

Minos – the scientific world where research and engineering is on-going. This is a domed world where humans live in giant atmospheric-controlled environments as the surface of the planet won't support human life.

Polara – the frozen world, an ice planet. While it has an atmosphere that supports native life, humans live in domes on it, only venturing out in heavy protective suits.

Etoria - One of the seven planets in the Astara system referred to as the Burning land, much like Venus is to Earth.

Ergos – another of the Astaran planets, rich with minerals, but not habitable. A few domes on it allow for temporary shelter for any teams who do extractions.

Deca – the water world. A continuous ocean, abundant with sea life, covers the planet.

RISING MAGEISTRA: RECALIBRATION

Heliotian Cycle Book Two

Lillian I. Wolfe

Chapter One

WHEN IN GYNZARA...

EYES BUGGING OUT, Travis DeLonghe gaped, mouth unhinged, at the humanoid figures as they approached. He, Maltron, and Bethayne hung back as Cynara and Linhok strode forward with quick, eager steps.

At nearly seven feet tall, these beings towered over all of them. Yet their bodies were like the slender reeds that grew in the pools near the ocean. Their paper-thin pale skin stretched tightly over gaunt frames, exaggerating every joint and muscle. Even their huge violet-blue eyes with no whites seemed unreal and out of proportion to the rest of their bodies. Rising like a halo around their oblong heads were long, feathery strands of white that resembled hair.

Travis swallowed hard. These Cantrese looked more alien than the Heliotians they'd left on the planet. He glanced at his companions and could tell by the befuddled expressions on their faces that they were as stunned as he was.

Still shocked, he watched numbly as Cynara hurried to greet them. When she stood face to face, she dropped to one knee, bowed her head, and kissed each offered hand, then, formalities over, rose and hugged each of them. The whole series of actions looked like they were performed in the air rather than touching the ground, so light were the movements.

Gravity, Travis concluded. Corlan's gravity was less than Arama's, so any movement could lift them into the air. His own steps had felt lighter, but he'd barely noticed it until now. He took a little hop and nearly fell when his body rose forward and up, challenging his balance. "Walk softly," he informed his companions. "Movement is easier here." They walked forward, adjusting with each step, to catch up with Cynara.

As they drew nearer, Travis noticed she faced the Cantrese and appeared to be conversing with them, but they exchanged no words

"Telepathy?" Maltron suggested, noting the same thing. "And we thought the Heliotians were strange."

"She said these were her people?" Bethayne questioned, her voice very low and awed.

"The Princess is half-Cantrese," Travis supplied, catching Bethayne's hand. "Her mother was human, but her father was one of these, although I can't for the life of me see how. Great Tiel, we can't be related in any way to them." He was in no way prepared for this. He'd seen no images of them in any of his schooling, and now he knew why. No wonder they didn't allow many humans to come to Corlan.

Behind the Controllers rose the elongated dome of the shuttle terminal. To Travis's eye, it resembled a vast beehive, but he guessed it to be at least three stories given the height of the Cantrese. Emerging from this building were dozens of others of the Clan, all looking much like the Controllers. They brought skimmers of some sort, larger than the ones used on Arama, with seating capacity for perhaps six each.

'They'll take care of our prisoners," Cynara explained as she returned to them. "Come on. Meet the people who saved our lives. They brought the shuttle in even though it's badly damaged."

The Controller, known as Kalrah, inclined his head slightly and spoke in Araman to them. His voice was soft, reedy, almost a whisper of the wind, nothing like the booming voice that had filled the shuttle pod. "It would not have been possible to control the shuttle if the Princess had not been on it. We could not gain access without a receiver on board. Thanks be to Tiel, we were able to intervene. We welcome you to Corlan. Please follow us."

Walking gingerly in the lighter atmosphere—Travis had already bounced almost three feet off the ground with too heavy a step—the group of humans set off behind the Controllers even as the skimmers whisked past them on the way to the shuttle. He shook his head in amusement. Those prisoners were in for even more of a surprise than he'd thought they would be.

"Other ships might be in pursuit," Cynara informed them as they walked. "My guess is they have a larger ship sitting somewhere out there, and those two came from it. If so, I'm sure they're wondering what has happened to the small ships they sent after us."

'The shield is still in place," Kalrah replied. "If they try to breach it, they will no longer be a problem. However, we have picked up no signs of a larger ship on any of our monitors, which means it would be quite far from our outrigger satellites."

"Or shielded somehow from it. Perhaps they have a way to appear invisible to our sensing equipment."

'But that's just a theory," Travis interjected, unable to contain his knowledge on this subject. "No one's worked out the technique for a blocking device."

She cast a sharp look at him. "It's a theory to us, but it may be a reality to them. If they can appear to be invisible on our tracking equipment, they could get quite close before we could get a visual on them."

Another Cantrese exited the building now and hurried, loose trousers flapping with the movement, toward them. Cynara looked up and smiled broadly. 'Savaith," she breathed so low that Travis barely caught the name. Then she broke into a run, her strides lifting her off the ground like an antelare springing. Still at her side, Linhok matched her strides with his smooth, graceful lope.

"Her father," Kalrah said as if it should be obvious.

Travis glanced at Damon, whose startled stare centered on the figure Cynara hugged, and shared his astonishment.

"How?" Damon asked.

Travis shrugged as his own thoughts surged. Cynara didn't look anything like these creatures, and she was raised here among these beings. Humans must have looked very peculiar to her after years of these.

As they caught up, Cynara introduced them to her father, then the Cantrese urged them to go into the dome. Once they passed the high door, the ceilings stretched nearly twice the height of the Cantrese. A circular stair at the curve opposite the one they came in led to the next level. The rounded structure extended to the furniture in the terminal and to the information and check-in desks. A dozen or so more Cantrese wandered or sat within the dome, but otherwise, the place was nearly empty. It looked large enough to accommodate hundreds.

When Travis commented on it, Cynara explained, "The Cantrese don't leave Corlan. This spaceport is exclusively for visitors from the planets, so not many Cantrese are here at any given time. And, since few visitors are allowed on Corlan, they don't need much staff. Long ago, there was a lot more travel between planets, and Corlan was a stopping place when humans first began to colonize the other planets, so the terminal was built to accommodate large numbers."

Travis nodded his understanding, but he began to realize there was a great deal he hadn't learned about the history of the planets and about the Clan of Cantra. He couldn't help but wonder why more wasn't programmed into Home Teacher. The colonization of the other planets rated only a few mentions, although it provided a fair amount of information about the construction of the domes.

Then there was the Clan, another area not covered. Were they once the same as the humans on Arama, and had they somehow evolved on Corlan to their present appearance, or were they always different? Why did they restrict travel to Corlan? Unable to stop himself, Travis stared again at Savaith. How could he possibly be Cynara's father?

The Controllers took their leave and started up the stairs to where their duty station was located. They had monitors there, they told them, and they would continue to observe for Heliotian ships.

Savaith directed them out to a waiting skimmer. Although spacious vertically, the seats were narrow and Travis, Bethayne, and Maltron fit snugly in the rear seat while Cynara sat up front next to her father. Linhok didn't jump inside, staring for a few moments at Cynara before he turned and struck out across the foliage-covered fields to the north.

"He'll meet us at my father's abode," Cynara said as she settled against the seat. "I have much to tell you, Savaith."

"I am sure you do," the Cantrese replied. His voice seemed no different from Kalrah's, slightly lower perhaps, but still very faint. "It can wait until we've reached home and you're refreshed."

She fell silent and leaned back to peer out the clear dome at her home world. Travis wondered what thoughts went through her mind as she gazed at it. *Had she missed it? Were her memories good, or had she struggled?*

From his view, Travis found it interesting, but it lacked the variety of Arama, where many different colors made up the landscape. Yet, it was very beautiful, and, as the princess had said, it was a peaceful-looking world.

“The colors are all a variant of blue… a little more red in this leaf to make a deep purple, a little less red in the grass to make it bright blue,” Maltron commented as he stared at the passing landscape.

“Maybe the atmosphere or the proximity to Astara must have affected the plant growth here,” Travis suggested.

In answer to his comment, Savaith spoke. "We control the colors of our plant life. The blue tones are soothing to our eyes; therefore, we've planned the shadings you see around you. Once, our eyes would tolerate a larger variety of colors, but no more."

“What changed?” Travis asked, curious why their physiology might change.

“We do not know exactly,” Savaith replied. “Perhaps our evolution or the change in the star system’s composition. It is of no great concern.”

Travis wanted to ask more, but Bethayne squeezed his hand and shook her head as if to tell him no. Perhaps she felt he was overstepping his place as a guest here. So, he sat back and watched the shades of blue and lavender flow past.

Secluded behind screens of the foliage, more domed buildings, not as large as the terminal they'd left but of the same general shape, rose into the pale sky. *Were these Cantrese homes and businesses? Did they even have the same kind of commerce as Arama?*

Savaith guided the skimmer through an opening in a hedge and stopped it in front of one of these hive-like structures. Ushering them inside, he gestured to the room to the right, where semi-circular chairs and a lounge formed a casual space. "Welcome. I will have refreshments brought. Please be comfortable." He removed his footwear and strode off toward what Travis presumed was the kitchen, leaving them to settle in their surroundings.

Following her father's example, Cynara removed her boots and set them next to his before stepping down into the room and sitting in one of the chairs. After a moment's hesitation, Maltron also took his boots off, lined them up, and went inside. Travis shrugged, glanced at Bethayne, and they followed the same actions. "As the old saying goes, when in Gynzara, do as the others do," he whispered, unexpectedly reminded of his own father, and he wondered what was happening at their farm.

Although the furniture sat higher than they were used to, Travis found it quite comfortable and relaxed into it. Within a few minutes, Savaith returned with a slightly shorter female Cantrese who brought Araman victuals, inviting them with a gesture to eat and drink.

Cynara barely ate any before she began relating the recent events on Arama. She told her father of her encounter with the aliens on the way to Tark Lonan. Travis watched him as his big eyes moved over himself, Damon, and Bethayne while she spoke about how she met each of them and their escape from Ama City. Savaith listened, his attention wandering as he sipped a cool drink and nibbled off one of the trays of fruits.

After she'd finished, he rose slowly, looking almost as if it were by magic rather than muscle power, and walked to the window to gaze out toward the sky. "You won't see the ship there, Savaith," Cynara said. "Nor can you sense it being there. I've tried. But I'm sure it is. The Heliotians could not have traveled here in those small ships."

Savaith turned back to her, and his eyes locked on hers. "Yes, I am sure you're correct. Now tell me, what is it you want, Daughter?"

About the Author

Lillian I. Wolfe

A sometimes musician, sporadic artist, occasional poet, and obsessed writer, Lillian Wolfe has spent most of her life writing something or the other. From fan fiction to short stories, novels, training manuals, newsletters, and other documentation, she has constantly been putting words on paper or a computer screen. She is, in fact, extremely grateful for the invention of the computer because using a manual typewriter is tedious. She loves all types of fiction, but her favorites are fantasy and mystery novels.

Lillian shares her home in northern Nevada with her best friend for the past thirty-odd years, three furry overlords—er—cats, and one feline-dominated toy poodle.

Other Books by This Author

Urban Fantasy

Funeral Singer Series

A Song for Marielle
A Song for Menafee
A Song of Betrayal
A Song of Forgiveness
A Song of Redemption

Science Fiction

O'Ceagan Saga Series

O'Ceagan's Legacy
In Strange Waters
Outer Rim

Time Threads Series

Time Walker
Splintered Time
Time Rewound (Coming in 2026)

Heliotian Cycle

Novice Mageistra : Broken Promises
Rising Mageistra: Recalibration (Winter 2026)

More From **Pynhavyn Press**
You might enjoy some of these books from our authors:

RENE AVERETT
Paranormal Cozy Mystery
Spotlight Sleuth Mysteries
A Trapdoor Tragedy- Novella Prequel
A Fatal Sweetness
A Harvest Moon Murder
A Drowning at the Maze
A Mask of Shadows (coming in late 2026)

Pembroke Mysteries
Scone Cold Murder (coming Soon)

ANGELINA FASANO
Urban Fantasy
Vampires Suck!
YA Urban Fantasy
Alpha's Song (Les Loupes Garou)
Beta Rising (Les Loups Garou)

RIONA KELLY
Romantic Suspense Fantasy
Cat Whisperer

Romantic Suspense
Bitter Vintage
Echoes of the Past – American Rose Abroad
Signature of a Soul – American Rose Abroad

RUSSELL D. JONES

Science Fiction
Orbital Strain
Gearforged: Undercity Scars Book 1

NICOLE FRENS

Urban Fantasy
CryoShift (Cryoverse Book 1)
Flight To Tomorrow: The CryoShift prequel short story (Cryoverse)

MARY WEATHERINGTON

Police Detective Mystery
For Eleven Million Reasons (Book 1)
$ide $wiped (Book 2)
The Gentle Giant Returns (Book 3)
Sometimes Love's Just Murder (Book 4)

CHILDREN'S BOOKS

By RENE AVERETT
Connie and the Missing Ladle –
Connie Cooks (K to 3rd)
Storm Squad Rising - (Mid-grade)

By ARLENE LLEWELLYN
(Illustrated by James Gayles)
Holly's Happy Heart (K to 3rd)

For updates on any books released through **Pynhavyn Press**, please visit our website and sign up on our mailing list. We only use this to notify you of any upcoming and imminent book releases.

www.pynhavynpress.com

www.ingramcontent.com/pod-product-compliance
Lightning Source LLC
LaVergne TN
LVHW031924090826
845145LV00018B/2825

* 9 7 8 1 9 4 2 6 2 2 3 7 6 *